Motel Mirrors

The Winter Foursome Sequel

By

Chad Wannamaker

Disclaimer

This story is intended for adult readers only. It contains explicit sexual content and is written to entertain and arouse. If graphic depictions of sexual situations offend you, please do not continue. This is a work of fiction. All names, characters, places, and events are fictional or used fictitiously. Any resemblance to actual persons, living or dead, businesses, events, or locations is purely coincidental.

ISBN: 978-1-7365913-9-0

This is a work of fiction. Names, characters, places, businesses, events, and incidents are either products of the author's imagination or are used fictitiously. Any resemblance to actual persons, living or dead, or actual events is purely coincidental.

EPISODE: 1: Splash

"Oh God, right there! Fuck, don't stop," Terry gasped, fingers gripping the luxurious sheets of the Four Seasons hotel bed like her life depended on it.

Donald didn't dare slow down. His tongue swirled faster, hungrier, tasting her fully as she arched beneath him. He relished the way her thighs clenched around his head, her hips bucking against his mouth. Her breath hitched sharply when he slipped two fingers inside her, curling them just the right way. He knew her now as well as he knew himself. The rhythm she craved, the pressure that unraveled her piece by piece.

"Fuck Donald, I'm gonna cum," Terry warned breathlessly, her hand tangling tightly in his hair.

He groaned softly against her, the vibration on her clit sending her spiraling over the edge. Terry's moan was raw and primal, her body shuddering violently beneath his touch. He didn't stop, savoring the taste and every pulse of her orgasm until she finally collapsed, breathless and trembling.

Slowly, he moved upward, pressing gentle kisses along her quivering belly, tasting the faint sheen of sweat on her skin. She looked up at him, eyes hazy with satisfaction and lingering heat.

"That was fucking incredible," Terry murmured, a smile spreading across her flushed face. She reached up, running her fingers down the firm muscles of his chest, biting her lower lip teasingly. "But what about you? Think you can handle more?"

Donald gave a low chuckle, leaning in until his lips hovered just above hers. "We've got plenty of time."

"Good," she purred softly, capturing his mouth in a deep, lingering kiss. "I taste good don't I? Tonight, I want every inch of you."

Donald didn't hesitate. He positioned himself carefully, watching Terry's face closely as he slowly pushed inside her. She gasped softly, her nails gently digging into his shoulders as she adjusted to his fullness. Her body rose to meet him, hips moving instinctively as they found their rhythm together.

"Fuck, you feel incredible," Donald murmured, his voice tight with restraint as he moved deeper, each thrust becoming more urgent, driven by mutual hunger.

"Yes, right there, babe. Don't stop," Terry whispered, wrapping her legs around him tightly, pulling him even closer, needing him fully.

"I'm not stopping. I love this pussy," he squeaked out.

The rhythmic sound of their skin smacking together was enhanced by her wetness spreading. He lost himself in the heat of her, the intensity building quickly, his control slipping.

"Fuck, I about to cum."

"Yes baby, fill me up. Please fill me up."

With a guttural moan, he finally let go, his body shuddering deeply as he emptied himself into her.

"Yes, I'm cumming again too! Keep pounding baby."

Their combined pleasure crashed over them like a wave, leaving them breathless and trembling together.

A brief chuckle filled the sexual air in the room. Their laughter was intimate, warm, a brief illusion of calm before the real world crept back in. They lay there for a moment, tangled and blissfully unaware of the storm they'd set in motion.

Finally, Donald rolled onto his back, one arm draped behind his head. "Think anyone at the bar recognized us?"

Terry laughed softly, propping herself up on one elbow, eyes gleaming mischievously. "If they did, they're definitely jealous now."

Donald smiled, but something in his chest tightened. The shadows of their past encounters flickered through his mind. Kristal's sly glances, and his uneasy situation with Peter and his hug cock. Pleasure came easily between him and Terry, but peace? Peace may never come.

Outside, footsteps shuffled softly down the hotel hallway, a quiet murmur, maybe laughter. Donald and Terry glanced at the door, then back at each other, smiles fading into cautious curiosity.

"Ready to face reality?" Terry asked quietly, fingers tracing slow, sensual circles on his chest.

Donald drew a slow breath, savoring the last few seconds of intimacy. "Not even a little. But this little roleplay was a nice break."

"Yeah, it was," Terry replied, looking down at the floor.

EPISODE: 2: The Group Chat

Donald stared at his phone like it had just slapped him.

Kristal [10:47 AM]:

"◈ who's ready for round 2? Summer house, Outer Banks, July 24–31. No excuses. Bring booze, swimsuits, and better secrets. 😘"

He reread it four times. Same winking emoji. Same cocky energy. Same Kristal.

Below it, Terry had already responded.

Terry [10:49 AM]:

"Oooooh yesss. I need sun and sin. We're in."

Well. That settled that.

Donald sighed and dropped the phone on the counter. Right next to it sat an unopened white bottle with shiny metallic labeling.

"Alpha Virility XL – For the Man You're Becoming."

It looked ridiculous sitting next to his clean protein shaker and the half-eaten banana he'd forgotten to finish after his morning workout.

He twisted the cap, stared into the bottle like it held answers, then sealed it again with a sigh.

Five months.

That's how long it had been since the Maine trip, since the mountain cabin, the hot tub, and the moaning through the goddamn walls. He still couldn't hear the words "Lift ticket" without feeling small.

Donald ran a hand down his face. He wasn't the same guy he was back then. Literally. Thirty pounds lighter, five days a week in the gym, meal-prepping like a bro in a shaker commercial. He even shaved his chest once, then scratched himself raw and swore never again.

The effort wasn't just about looking better. It was about not feeling like the punchline of someone else's fantasy. Mainly, his wife's fantasy.

Terry hadn't really said a thing about his transformation. She noticed, and sure she'd said some vague things like "you look leaner" in the middle of folding laundry. But it wasn't the way he needed her to notice.

He glanced at the toaster's reflection. Jawline? Visible. Neck? Present. Arms? Not bad, if he flexed just right.

Still, something was missing. Maybe it was size. Maybe it was swagger. Maybe it was just confidence, and the pills promised to manufacture that too.

"You gonna keep modeling or clean the damn blender?" Terry's voice broke his spiral.

He turned around. She walked in, fresh from her run, glowing, dewy, beautiful in that effortless way that made him simultaneously proud and panicked. Her sports bra clung to her curves. Her dark curls were damp and pulled into a loose ponytail. Even her sweat looked sexy to him.

"Sorry," he said, grabbing the blender like it had committed a crime. "Just reading Kristal's message. So, Outer Banks, huh? Think it's a good idea?"

"Yep." Was Terry's simple answer as she opened the fridge, grabbed a bottle of water, and leaned against the door like a scene from a wellness ad. "Should be fun. Beach this time. Change of scenery."

The she smiled a little too brightly for Donald's liking.

"Maybe this trip won't be so... intense," she added.

Donald forced a grin. "Right. Fun in the sun. Group therapy with sunscreen."

Terry rolled her eyes. "We're all adults. So, don't worry."

Donald didn't respond.

As Terry moved past him, her fingers traced the curve of his back, gentle and familiar. Not icy. Not thrilling. Just warm. Their roleplay hadn't lit the spark they were chasing. Instead, it left a soft burn, like coals that never quite caught fire."

Once she disappeared into the bathroom, he stared at the counter again. His phone buzzed.

Kristal [10:59 AM]:

"BTW I invited two extras this time 😏 You'll love them. Going to be epic. Promise."

Two extras? He narrowed his eyes. Kristal didn't promise anything unless she was stirring the pot. He had a feeling she'd been shaking the whole damn spice rack.

Donald picked up the supplement bottle again, and the label practically winked at him.

He muttered the caption, "Enhance your confidence. Dominate your desire."

"Dominate my damn bills," he thought with a smile. Then, he unscrewed the cap.

The garage gym wasn't fancy, but it was his. Adjustable bench. A full rack. Dumbbells. A punching bag that hadn't been used in weeks but it made him feel badass with it just hanging there.

Donald threw on some music, old-school hip-hop and started his warm-up. Pushups, pull-ups, and some light curls to the rhythm helped slow his thoughts. He used to be proud of his body. Not because it was perfect, because it got shit done. However, Maine had shaken that.

Peter's body. Peter's confidence. Peter's everything.

Even now, Donald couldn't forget Terry watching Peter fix that damn heat lamp. Her eyes had drifted and stayed. He'd noticed. And done nothing.

That's what stung. Not her looking, he got it, Peter was a walking thirst trap. It was the silence afterward. The unspoken parts. The way Terry had never brought it up.

That, and Kristal's noises through the walls.

Donald grunted mid-rep, forcing the weights up like he could bench-press the memory away.

After his workout, Donald sat at the kitchen table with a towel over his shoulders, staring out the window. Terry was outside now, watering the plants. Her tank top clung to her back, and he let himself admire her for a moment.

She was still the woman he'd fallen for. Still smart, sexy, sarcastic in all the right ways. But they hadn't been in sync in weeks, months.

Hell, maybe longer.

The Maine trip had just exposed the cracks that were already there. Like a spotlight on the things, they didn't say. About attraction. About curiosity. About how comfortable they'd gotten and not in the sexy way, but the lazy way.

His phone buzzed again.

This time, a private message.

Kristal [11:03 AM]:

"BTW bring swim trunks that actually fit this time. 😏 Beach bodies are coming for blood lol."

Donald stared at the screen. Was that flirting? Friendly banter? Or was she hinting at what hadn't happened in Maine?

Back at the cabin, there was a moment between them. In the kitchen, alone, too many drinks. She'd leaned close and whispered something about "seeing potential." He'd laughed it off, but she didn't.

Maybe it was time he stopped laughing everything off.

Later that night, Terry stood in front of the bedroom mirror, trying on a swimsuit. She twisted left, then right, admiring the cut. Donald watched from the bed, quietly.

"That new?" he asked.

"Yeah. Figured I'd go bold for the beach." She smiled, but not at him.

"You look amazing in it," he said. Soft, sincere.

She paused. "Thanks." No follow-up. No compliment back. Just "thanks."

She turned back to the mirror. Donald stood up, walked behind her, and wrapped his arms around her waist. He kissed her shoulder. She didn't pull away, but she didn't melt either.

He whispered, "You ever think about that night? The last trip?"

Terry stiffened just slightly. "You mean the orgasm symphony next door?"

He chuckled. "Yeah. That. All of it. How... crazy it got."

She met his eyes in the mirror. "It was a moment. We're past it."

"Are we?" he asked.

She held his gaze. "Do you want to go down that road again?"

"I'm not sure we ever left it."

She turned around, placing a hand on his chest. "I love you, Donald. That hasn't changed."

"I know," he said.

But something had shifted. That love that they had didn't look the same.

That night, they lay in bed facing opposite directions. Donald stared at the door, wide awake, while Terry's breathing settled into rhythm.

He reached for his phone. Another message from Kristal had come in hours ago, but he hadn't seen it.

Kristal [2:11 PM]:

"It's Nia and Julian that's coming. Not much of a surprise I know, but they couldn't come last time. Trust me. This trip's gonna be different."

Donald read it twice. Then again. And again.

Something told him different didn't mean easier.

Terry shifted in her sleep beside him. Donald listened to the slow rhythm of her breath, the soft rasp of the ceiling fan stirring air above them. Their bedroom smelled faintly of lemongrass and fabric softener clean, cozy, and quiet. Too quiet.

He checked his phone again.

Midnight.

He rolled onto his back, stared at the ceiling, and whispered, "What am I doing wrong?"

The silence didn't answer.

There was a time when Terry would have turned into him in her sleep. She used to rest her leg over his, tuck her foot under his calf like a secret. Now she stayed on her side, distant but not angry—just... separate.

They hadn't fought. That was the weird part. If they'd screamed at each other, it might've been easier. Instead, they'd drifted, silently, like boats tied to different docks.

His phone buzzed one more time an Instagram notification.

@NiaJKnowsBest tagged you in a story.

He blinked. What the hell does she want?

He tapped it open.

A quick selfie video: Kristal and Nia clinking glasses at some outdoor rooftop lounge. Nia, presumably, was laughing with her phone held high, while Kristal mouthed something to the camera.

"The boys aren't ready," she lip-synced dramatically. "Not even close."

The clip ended with Kristal biting her lip and Nia winking.

Donald sat up.

"Well. Okay then."

He clicked on Nia's profile to look at more of her recent pictures.

One photo was of her in a gold bikini that did not leave anything to the imagination. He briefly read over Nia's profile, a fashion publicist from Brooklyn. He glanced at a few pictures. There were several of her and Terry; Kristal.

Donald shut the app quickly, suddenly feeling warm. Not because he was interested in Terry's friend, at least not entirely, but because he knew how this game worked. Kristal was setting the stage. Luring attention. Priming the drama before they ever crossed the state line.

And Terry had already RSVP'd "Yes."

The next morning, Donald woke to find Terry scrolling on her phone beside him. Her hair was a puff of gorgeous chaos against the pillow, and she looked good, soft and rested.

"Morning," he mumbled.

"Morning," she replied without looking up.

"What's got your attention this early?"

She smiled slightly. "Nia. That girl... she's wild. She just posted a reel talking about orgasms and warm pretzels."

Donald blinked. "What?"

"I know. She's hilarious though. Definitely going to be the life of the trip." She laughed softly. "Might even teach you something."

He ignored that last bit and sat up.

Terry kept scrolling, thumb moving with idle pleasure.

"I'm thinking about packing early," she said. "I want to look good this time."

Donald didn't say anything. What he wanted to ask was: For who?

Later that afternoon, he stood at the sink, rinsing his blender bottle, shirtless, when he caught a glimpse of himself in the window's reflection. He flexed. The line of his deltoid caught the light just right. It wasn't Peter's physique, but it wasn't nothing either.

The front door opened, and Kristal's voice shouted from the hallway.

"Knock, knock! I brought tequilaaaa!"

Donald blinked. "What the hell?"

Terry jogged out of the bedroom. "She's just dropping something off. Chill."

Kristal walked in with oversized sunglasses, cutoff shorts, and a tank top that required real commitment. She looked like vacation had already started.

"I figured we'd pregame before the beach, metaphorically speaking," she said, holding up the bottle.

Donald gave her a tight smile. "Starting early."

She looked him over and raised a brow. "Well damn. Someone's been doing pull-ups in private. Look at you."

Terry smirked. "He's been living in the garage gym."

Donald blushed, muttering something about protein.

Kristal sauntered closer, leaned against the counter, and tapped the supplement bottle sitting next to the sink.

"Still chasing that alpha energy, huh?" she teased. "You might be dangerous this time."

Donald gave her a lopsided grin. "Or I might just be tired and sore. We'll see."

Kristal leaned in, close enough for Donald to smell coconut oil and mischief. "Something tells me... this trip's gonna light a few fires."

Then she winked, turned on her heel, and left the bottle on the counter before strolling out of the kitchen.

Terry grabbed the tequila and laughed. "She's chaos. But she does keep things interesting."

"Yeah," he said, more to himself. "She definitely does."

Donald stared after her.

EPISODE: 3: Check-In & First Glances

The beach house stood tall like it knew it was the main character. Three floors, wraparound decks, whitewashed siding, and the kind of panoramic view you didn't get unless you were rich, lucky, or Kristal.

Donald pulled into the gravel driveway, the crunch under the tires oddly satisfying. The ocean was only a few hundred feet away beautiful, sparkling, endless.

"Damn," he muttered.

Terry, wearing oversized sunglasses and a straw hat tilted just right, leaned forward to look. "Kristal did not come to play."

"She rarely does," Donald replied, shifting into park.

Kristal's Jeep was already there, as was a matte black Mercedes coupe Donald didn't recognize.

"Guess we're not the first," he said.

"Good. I need a drink and a breeze," Terry replied as she unclipped her seatbelt.

The house smelled like citrus and ocean salt when they walked in. It was an open floor plan, modern furniture, and just enough beachy decor to say yes, I'm coastal, without screaming I shop at HomeGoods.

Kristal emerged from the kitchen wearing denim shorts, a crop top, and a margarita. She squealed when she saw Terry.

"You made it!" She ran up and hugged her, spilling half her drink. "My girl, looking all sexy-travel-chic!"

Terry laughed, hugging her back.

"And you look like trouble."

"Always," Kristal purred, then turned to Donald. "Oh shit, the new and improved Donald. You've been doing crunches and pushups and shit with those pullups, haven't you?"

"I lift things. Occasionally." Donald chuckled awkwardly.

Kristal gave him a slow once-over. More intense than before. "Well, color me impressed. Your arms are giving hot dad energy. I like it."

Terry side-eyed her but said nothing.

Donald shifted his bag to his other shoulder. "Who else is here?"

Kristal gestured toward the stairs. "Peter just went to set up the rooftop bar. And Nia's somewhere unpacking her seventeen outfits for a week. Girl brought a trunk. I swear she thinks we're filming a reality show."

Terry arched a brow. "I mean... are we not?"

Before anyone could answer, a voice called from upstairs.

"I brought options because I like to have range!"

Nia descended the stairs in high-waisted linen pants, a barely-there top, and enough jewelry to catch the light with every step. Nia Jameson was glowing, bronze skin, curly auburn hair pulled into a loose bun, and a smirk that dared anyone to underestimate her.

"Hey Terry," she said, extending a hand with perfectly manicured nails.

"Hey Nia. Good to see you," Terry said, shaking it. "And this is—"

"Donald," Nia interrupted, looking him up and down. "The improved husband. Mmm." She grinned. "Nice to meet the man behind the blender bottles and protein posts."

"Uh. Thanks?" Donald laughed

Kristal laughed. "Nia's a professional flirter, now. You'll get used to it."

Nia winked. "Oh honey, I'm just warming up."

"Yeah, we all know," Terry interjected.

"So, where's Peter," Donald asked nonchalantly.

Kristal rolled her eyes, "Upstairs unpacking I guess."

"Hmm, guess we should get to that too babe," Terry said looking at Donald.

The rest of the check-in went fast. Rooms were chosen; Terry and Donald took the second-floor suite with a balcony; Kristal and Peter claimed the rooftop connecting rooms; Nia got the room closest to the kitchen.

Donald unpacked quickly. He brought less this time. More tank tops. More swim trunks that actually fit. And only one pair of jeans, because he was determined to stay in the sun, not the shadows.

Terry was on the balcony, sipping sparkling water and staring at the waves. Donald walked up behind her and wrapped an arm around her waist.

She didn't pull away, but she didn't lean in either.

"You okay?" he asked.

"Yeah," she said. "Just decompressing. It's been a long few months."

He nodded. "It really has."

They stood like that for a moment, quiet.

Then Terry said, "Do you think this trip will be different?"

Donald thought about Peter. About Kristal. About the pills in his toiletry bag.

“I think,” he said slowly, “It’s gonna be unforgettable. One way or another.”

"Hmm," was the only response to his statement.

Late that afternoon, a new car pulled into the driveway, a sleek black Audi. Donald spotted it through the blinds while changing into shorts.

“That must be Julian,” Terry called from the bathroom, already applying a layer of sunscreen.

Donald didn’t reply.

He headed downstairs and opened the front door just as Julian was grabbing his suitcase from the trunk.

Julian was tall. Roughly 6’2”. Lean. Golden-brown skin. Sharp jawline. He wore a plain white tee, joggers, and low-top sneakers, but somehow made it look designer.

“Yo!” Julian called out with a smile. “House of sin and sand, I presume?”

Donald grinned despite himself. “Yeah man. Welcome to the madness. I'm Donald.”

"I'm Julian."

They shook hands. Julian’s grip was firm, warm. Confident without trying.

“Place is crazy,” he said, looking up at the balconies. “Kristal said beachfront, but this is some movie shit.”

“She doesn’t do subtle.” Donald replied.

Terry walked out, still in her shorts and bikini top. “Hey, Jules!”

Julian’s face lit up. “T! Damn, you look great.”

They hugged. A little too long. Donald crossed his arms, forcing a smile.

“So, you two know each other?” he asked.

"Yeah, we worked on that diabetes campaign last year," Terry said. "Did the whole shoot in Charleston."

"Oh yeah," Julian added. "Terry saved the whole project. She got the client to stop insisting on plastic palm trees."

Terry laughed. "And you refused to wear shoes the whole week."

"Shoes are oppressive, T," Julian replied.

They laughed but Donald didn't.

Later, on the back patio, the group gathered for drinks. The sun was low, and the ocean breeze soft and sticky. The grill fired up, Peter's doing, and the cooler was packed with beer, White Claw, and Nia's special sangria, which smelled like hangover and regret.

Kristal played bartender, Nia DJ'd from a Bluetooth speaker, and Peter mingled. He was watching everything like he was calculating how much he could say before things spiraled. Thoughts of Kristal, Terry and the previous trip were running through his mind.

Terry sat next to Julian, their heads close as they talked about Charleston and creative campaigns. Kristal sat across from them, smirking behind her margarita. Nia watched with amused detachment.

Donald took the seat next to Kristal and cracked open a beer. She leaned in.

"Vibes are wild already," she whispered.

He nodded.

"You holding up okay?" she asked.

He looked at Terry and Julian laughing again. Then, back to Kristal.

"Ask me again tomorrow."

Kristal touched his thigh under the table, just briefly.

"Don't worry," she said. "You'll have options too."

After dinner, the group naturally split, some lounging around the outdoor fire pit, others slipping inside for drinks or showers. Donald stayed outside, sipping a whiskey and nursing the ache in his shoulders from his earlier pushup session.

Kristal curled up on the outdoor couch beside him, barefoot, hair in a loose knot, still radiant. She looked over her glass of sangria and gave him a slow grin.

"You always this quiet?" she asked.

"Only when everyone else is loud."

Kristal chuckled. "Fair. But you used to be louder."

"I did?" He raised a brow.

"You've been quiet since the last trip. Even now, with those new shoulders and that chest, you're...watching." She leaned in slightly. "You still feel like the side character, huh?"

He didn't answer, but the flicker in his expression said plenty.

Kristal tapped his thigh again.

"You know, most people don't realize it, but quiet ones are the ones you gotta watch out for. They're the ones who surprise you."

Donald took a sip of his drink and looked out at the waves.

"Maybe I'm done surprising people."

"Nah. You're just getting started."

Inside, Nia had changed into a sleek black romper with dramatic gold earrings. She leaned against the kitchen island, watching Julian mix a drink with surgical precision.

"You bartend in your off hours, or just seduce professionally?" she asked, amused.

Julian flashed a grin. "A little of column A, a little of column B."

Terry laughed from across the kitchen. "He was everyone's favorite during the Charleston shoot. Even the interns blushed."

"Interns have taste," Nia said.

Kristal came in behind them, voice loud and dramatic. "Okay, okay, okay. We're not doing a whole 'get-to-know-you' night without a game. I won't allow it."

"Oh god," Terry said, already groaning. "Just, don't."

Kristal pointed. "Yes. We're doing it. Icebreaker time. But make it hot."

"Define hot," Julian said.

Kristal grinned. "Fast paced. Flirty. And if you lie, you drink."

Donald walked in then, clearly catching the end of the threat.

"What game is this?" he asked.

Nia answered, "It's called 'Sip or Strip Your Soul.' Trademark pending."

Julian laughed. "Sounds like a lawsuit."

They all gathered back around the fire pit, this time closer, drinks in hand. The night air had cooled just enough to make things cozy.

Kristal clasped her hands.

"Okay. First round. Rules are simple: Answer the question honestly or take a big sip. And I mean a big one. Don't be cute." She looked around the circle. "First question," she said, locking eyes with Terry. "If you could sleep with anyone here, besides your current partner, who would it be?"

Donald blinked.

Julian raised his brows and let out a low whistle.

Terry hesitated just a beat too long.

“I’ll sip,” she said finally, and downed a healthy pour of sangria.

“Oh, scandalous.” Nia clapped.

Kristal moved on. “Julian—same question.”

Julian leaned back, grinning.

“Well, I'm single but honestly? Probably Nia. I feel like she’d break my heart and take my car, but I’d still thank her.”

“That’s pretty fucking accurate.” Nia laughed.

“Donald,” Kristal said, turning her full attention on him.

He didn’t look at Terry. He looked directly at Kristal.

“If I weren’t married?” he asked.

"Yeah, sure. That still counts," Kristal nodded.

“I’d want to be wanted,” he said. “Whoever that ended up being with.”

For a moment, the entire group was quiet. Even Nia tilted her head, surprised.

Terry shifted in her seat, sipping again without a word.

“Damn,” Kristal murmured. “Well played, Sir.”

"Peter, how about you?"

"Well, I'm technically single too, so I don’t know. I guess keeping options open isn’t an answer. Right? So, I'll just take a drink."

"Okay, I guess that's that then," Kristal said as her perpetual smile melted.

"Nia?"

"I'd say Julian. Seems like he gets me."

"What about you?" Peter asked Kristal

"I would say...I'm taking a fucking drink."

"Hmm, figures," Peter muttered.

Later that night, the house settled into its separate spaces—bedrooms and balconies, whispered conversations and laughter drifting down the halls.

Donald lay in bed, staring at the ceiling again. While Terry was beside him, scrolling on her phone in silence.

"Julian seems cool," he said casually.

Terry nodded. "He's fun. Chill. Easy to talk to." Donald didn't push the conversation, but she added, "We're just friends."

He turned his head to look at her. "Are we?"

That caught her by surprise. Terry looked over, phone lowering slowly.

"What's that supposed to mean, Donald?"

"It means... I don't know where we are anymore," he said. "I'm working out. Trying. Pushing. But we still feel like strangers. And I'm not even sure if you miss me."

She exhaled. "Donald of course I do. I really don't feel like talking about this. But since you insist, something broke in you in Maine. And I don't know if either of us can figure out what. I mean do we even want the same things anymore? Things were fine there, but as soon as we left..."

He nodded slowly, not speaking a word. Not knowing how to finish her sentence either. They lay there, the silence saying more than their words ever could.

^An Hour Later...^

Downstairs, Kristal stood at the kitchen counter, eating cold grapes out of a plastic bag. She wore an oversized tee and no bra; her hair piled on top of her head in a loose knot.

Donald walked in shirtless, clearly unable to sleep. He grabbed a water bottle and leaned against the counter opposite her.

"Couldn't sleep?" she asked.

"Nope."

Kristal tossed a grape in the air and caught it with her mouth. "Terry?"

"Always."

She nodded, chewing.

"It's exhausting, isn't it? Feeling like someone's slipping away and not knowing if you should chase them or let them go."

Donald didn't respond.

Kristal popped another grape. "I've been there. Chased until my legs gave out. Then I realized, maybe I wasn't supposed to catch them."

He looked at her. "Is that what you're doing now? Not chasing Peter?"

Kristal smiled, sad and sharp. "Maybe, I'm just tired of chasing things that don't want to be caught."

Then there was a pause. A quiet truce between their ghosts. Her thoughts about the fun times with Peter contrasted with the bad.

Kristal reached across the counter and flicked him a grape from her bag.

"You're stronger than you think. In every way. Even the ones that don't matter."

He nodded, twisted the cap off his water and took a drink to wash down the grape.

"Get some sleep, Donald. Try not to dream about me too much," she said with a smile.

EPISODE: 4: Beneath the Surface

The next morning came in on a breeze that smelled like salt and second chances.

Donald was already up, jogging along the shoreline barefoot. The sand gritted under his heels, wet and cool from the tide that had rolled in hours earlier. He didn't run for speed. He ran to outrun his thoughts, at least for a little while.

The past twenty-four hours had twisted something in him. Not in a painful way, exactly. But in the way an old joint clicks into place after being out of alignment for too long. Unsettling but necessary.

He ran until the house shrank behind him. Then turned around and jogged back, breathing hard, chest slick with sweat, lungs stretched but clear.

Kristal was already outside when he reached the deck. She was barefoot, in a sports bra, shorts, and sipping iced coffee. She raised her cup in greeting.

"Damn. Look at you all sweaty and useful."

"Gotta keep the transformation arc consistent." Donald said as his breath caught.

"Well, you're on pace to make someone mad horny or mad jealous. Either way, I approve."

"Guess I'll, uhh... try not to trip over my own charm," Donald replied as he stepped past her, forcing a nervous chuckle.

The way her eyes lingered wasn't teasing anymore; it was consideration. And Donald wasn't sure he could handle that right now.

By noon, everyone had gathered on the beach. It was a hotter day, the kind of heat that made the air shimmer and forced even the most stylish to abandon fashion for function.

Donald wore black swim trunks and a loose tank. Kristal had on a white bikini under a purple sheer wrap. Peter kept his shades on and barely spoke, the hangover taking his words. Nia was in a neon green two-piece that practically glowed. And Julian wore coral board shorts and a smile that could sell sex and sunscreen in equal measure.

Terry wore the same bikini she'd packed on the winter trip and a matching sarong tied low on her hips. It was deliberate but not slutty.

Donald watched her settle on a towel beside Julian, close but not touching. That invisible thread of jealousy was back. The one that tugged a little tighter every time one of them laughed or looked just a second too long.

Kristal tossed Donald a bottle of sunscreen. "Unless you're trying to come back looking like beef jerky, I suggest you lather up."

Donald caught it, grinning. "You offering to help?"

She raised a brow. "You offering to moan my name like you mean it this time?"

Julian nearly choked on his water.

Terry rolled her eyes, but she was smiling.

"Oh, this trip's about to be messy, messy," Nia muttered.

Kristal patted the towel behind him. "Turn."

He did. Cool lotion hit his shoulders; her palms moved slow, sure, working circles into the knots at his traps. He held his breath without meaning to.

"Relax," she murmured near his ear, almost a laugh. "SPF fifty and bad decisions."

Her thumbs traced the lines of his lats, skimming down his sides, stopping just shy of the waistband. A shiver betrayed him.

Terry broke her conversation with Julian to look, looked away, adjusted her sarong like it needed adjusting, then continued her conversation.

Peter tipped his shades down a millimeter, "You can rub a little on me too."

Kristal just gave him a cold look. "Flip. You want your chest too?" Kristal asked Donald, tapping his shoulder.

"I'm good," he said, voice lower than he intended.

She capped the bottle with a neat pop. "Sure. Save the front for later."

Donald didn't answer.

Hours passed under the sun's lazy burn. Some people swam while others relaxed with books, umbrellas and oversized hats. House music thumped quietly from a Bluetooth speaker.

Donald sat near the water, letting it lap over his toes. He hadn't spoken much to anyone. He just watched when Terry and Julian would interact.

Peter barely acknowledged Kristal's actions toward him. He spent more time tossing a football with Julian, staring at Terry or texting someone. Kristal, for her part, didn't chase after him. She joked, flirted, bantered but she didn't reach for Peter.

Nia was everywhere, chatting, filming, taking selfies, and hyping everyone up. She slowed when she walked past Donald, giving him a once-over and murmuring, "Now that's an improvement project with potential."

Donald looked up and chuckled. "I didn't know I was under renovation."

"You were," she said plainly. "Now? You might be ready for listing."

"Okay, but no price drops."

Donald laughed and went back to looking at the ocean as Nia continued her journey. The hours passed by, and day began to give way to dusk.

"Guess I'm going to head back. I need a shower." Terry said to Julian in whisper.

Kristal heard her and announced, "I think we should take this party to the roof!"

Back at the house, after showers and cold drinks, everyone reassembled around the rooftop bar Peter had stocked earlier.

Kristal played DJ this time, bossa nova melting into R&B, then into sexy late-2000s throwbacks. The mood turned golden.

Terry mixed a round of drinks. It was something with passionfruit, mint, and vodka. She passed them out to everyone. When she got to Donald she passed it without meeting his eyes.

He took a sip. "It's good. Really good."

"Yeah, thanks. It's the same thing I made for you last summer."

"Really?"

Terry finally looked at him and let out a deep sigh.

"Yeah, really. You liked it then too."

The blank statement made something warm and painful flare in his chest. He nodded and quietly walked to the edge of the deck.

Behind him, Kristal was laughing with Terry and Nia. Peter stood off to the side, talking to Julian about some work thing. But Donald felt like he was underwater.

Then he heard Kristal say, "He's changing. You can see it."

"Yeah. But who knows what people will fit in that change." Terry's voice answered, quiet but audible.

The words hit Donald square in the ribs. He didn't flinch. He didn't move. He just sipped his drink and let the ocean air numb the sting. Nia glanced at Donald to see if he heard what Terry said, then changed the conversation to looking for a new car.

The sun had dipped low enough to paint the sky in strokes of lavender and fire-orange by the time anyone suggested food.

Terry and Julian volunteered to head into town for food and more mixers. Donald didn't object, but he noticed the way she didn't ask him to ride along.

Once the car pulled away, Nia reappeared from the kitchen with a bong in one hand and a bowl of grapes in the other.

"Beach law," she said, lighting up. "If you're still sad after two days, you get high, hydrated, and half-naked until you forget why."

Kristal took a long drag from the bong, then passed it to Donald without hesitation.

"Seriously?" he blinked.

"You need to relax. One puff won't undo your protein gains," Nia said. She laughed, lounging back with the grapes tucked under her chin like a hedonistic goddess. “Honestly, if you don’t want it pass it to me. I got weed for days.”

"What the hell," Donald said as he took the bong and inhaled. He took a light, smooth drag. His throat scratched on the exhale, and he coughed once, grinning.

“Damn,” he rasped. “Alright, now I feel like I’m on vacation.”

“That’s the spirit.” Kristal winked.

Around 9 p.m., the car pulled back in. Terry and Julian returned carrying bags of oysters, scallops, cocktail shrimp, and wine like they were prepping for a reality show cook-off.

"We got the goods," Julian yelled as they walked to the house.

"About time. Did you guys have to go fishing?" Peter yelled back with a laugh.

He hopped down the steps to help them bring it all inside.

Julian popped the trunk. “Yo, you ever had Carolina-style firecracker scallops?”

“Nope,” Peter said.

“Tonight’s your lucky night, my man.”

They made their way inside the kitchen and dropped the bags on the counter. Terry grabbed a pack of basil and set it beside the stove. Her face was glowing from the wine and her eyes were glassy. She seemed a little more occupied than usual.

“You okay?” Donald asked quietly.

She nodded, not looking up.

“Yeah. Just... thinking.”

“About?”

Terry shrugged. “How hard it is to be in love with someone who makes you feel safe but not excited.”

Donald's throat dried.

"You talking about me?" he asked.

"I don't know." She finally met his gaze. "Maybe, I'm just talking."

He nodded, stepping back, giving her space.

"Well, talking is good. Can't know what someone is thinking without it."

Julian cracked open a beer behind them, oblivious to the situation. "Hey, you guys making food in here, or fucking."

Terry looked around Donald, "Jules, get the fuck out of the kitchen, please."

Julian chuckled and walked back outside.

Peter was at the edge of the hallway, with a towel around his neck, watching it all.

Dinner became a blur of rich food and heavier wine. Everyone loosened up laughing harder, leaning closer. Even Peter cracked a few more smiles, though his eyes never lingered too long on Kristal. Donald stayed mostly quiet, sipping his drink and laughing at other conversations.

"Oysters are just expensive foreplay in a shell." Kristal said, twirling one on her fork.

Everyone laughed except Terry, who looked down at her plate, smile flickering.

"Well, that explains why Peter always goes straight for the main course," Nia quipped, raising her glass. "No patience for the build-up."

The table cracked up. Donald spit out his wine.

Peter leaned back, lazy grin returning. "No patience? The only thing I rush is her first orgasm. Second one waits till she says my name right."

Laughter broke around the table again. Nia clinked his glass.

Terry glanced at Peter's crotch, blinked twice and sipped. Donald's knuckles whitened around the stem of his glass when he saw the glance.

Later, as dishes were cleared and people peeled off to their corners, Donald took his drink and found a quiet spot on the balcony. He was resting on the railing twirling his drink, face bathed in moonlight.

Kristal saw him and decided to walk over.

"You okay?" she asked softly.

"Yeah, I'm good. I'm just getting used to this...new thing that's happening."

Kristal stepped closer, her voice low and uncharacteristically serious.

"You know sometimes we overthink new things because change is hard. The loss of control is what we have to get used too. You're more than what was lost, you know. You could be what someone's hoping to find."

He turned to her, and for a long moment, nothing passed between them but the sound of the waves.

Finally, she patted him on the shoulder, "Come inside or stay out here, but Donald, don't just stand in the doorway."

She kissed him on the arm and walked inside.

EPISODE: 5: Open Bar, Closed Doors

"Tonight is not a stay here and be weird night. Fuck that, we're going out. I want sweat, neon lights, ruthless decisions, and zero regrets." Nia declared before noon.

"You had me at ruthless decisions." Kristal grinned.

Julian started searching for local spots. "There's a few places in town that stay open late. And they all have karaoke. Sundogs website shows they have live music too. The reviews say strong drinks."

"Dress code?" Peter looked up from his tablet.

"Smart casual. So basically: wear pants and don't smell like weed."

"I make no promises," Nia replied, twirling in her bikini wrap.

Donald sat at the kitchen island, sipping a protein shake, trying not to make it obvious he was staring at Terry. She was standing at the sink, laughing at something Kristal said about tequila and trust issues. She looked happy and comfortable in her skin in a way that both hurt and excited him.

He hated that he noticed every damn thing about her still. How she always tapped her nail against her glass when she was about to say something uncomfortable. How she never quite smiled with her full mouth unless they were alone.

By evening, the house had turned into a dressing room. Donald was looking in the mirror at his upgraded physique. He gently stroked his cock to get a rise so he could see what it looked like against his abs.

Peter was in the bathroom having a jerkoff fest to old videos of him and Kristal.

Kristal's playlist thumped from the Bluetooth speaker. It had all the women singing along between sips of wine.

"Damn, Terry," Nia said, holding up a backless green dress with a devilish grin. "This with that sculpted back. You'll cause a scene."

Terry hesitated, eyeing it like it might bite. "It's a lot of back."

Kristal smirked from the vanity mirror, touching up her lip gloss. "Girl, it's just skin. Let 'em see what clean living and Pilates built."

"I don't know. Maybe but it's not my usual."

"Usual is overrated," Nia replied with a laugh.

After a few more protests and a little wine, Terry finally gave in.

"Alright, alright. I'll wear the damn dress," Terry said with a smile as she took it from Kristal. "You know," she said looking in the mirror, "I do look hot in this don't I."

Kristal and Nia both laughed. "Damn right!"

When they all walked downstairs ten minutes later, Julian let out a slow, appreciative whistle from the living room.

"Okay, green goddess," he said, clapping once. "Somebody warn the bartenders."

Terry laughed, her cheeks warming up. "Y'all are too much."

Donald came down next, adjusting the collar of his charcoal button-up. The fit was snug in the chest and arms, and his black jeans were crisp. He headed to the kitchen to grab a drink. Kristal's gaze followed him. "Damn," she said casually, pouring tequila into a glass. "You clean up better than I remember."

"It's the shirt. Or maybe it shrunk when I washed it."

Kristal laughed. "Or maybe you finally stopped dressing like a divorced math teacher."

He chuckled and shook his head, but his ears started to warm from the banter as he grabbed a lime wedge from the counter.

"I mean, somebody came to cause problems," she said, part-laughing, part-praising.

"You think this says trouble?" he asked, tugging at the collar.

"Well, maybe not trouble as much as it says purposeful glow-up. I like it." Kristal leaned in.

"Yeah, he looks great," Terry interjected in a cold tone, stopping the banter.

Peter came down last. He wore slim-fit slacks, minimal cologne, and a fitted blue shirt. There was a silent tension in his wake.

"Okay, I see you there big fella," Nia called out to Peter.

"Eh, it's just something I threw together. You know, a simple late night." Peter replied, giving a smile.

Kristal looked at him and rolled her eyes. They were trying to make a friendship work, but sometimes a pang of antagonism would sting her.

Julian clapped his hands.

"Okay, you beautiful, chaotic people, let's go make memories we'll argue about tomorrow."

They piled out of the house slowly and began their journey for the evening.

The bar was nice with a simple style. It was everything the website promised.

Dim lights, velvet booths and some tables. It had a rooftop view with a pool, but no one was allowed to swim. A DJ was in the corner playing house remixes like he was born in Ibiza. There were string lights, and a general air of you better act like you belong there.

Kristal and Nia disappeared immediately, heading straight to the side bar like queens reclaiming their thrones. Terry stuck close to Julian at the main bar, laughing as he tried to decode the signature cocktail names.

Donald and Peter stayed in the back. Donald wasn't awkward anymore, but he still didn't know what role he was playing tonight. Husband? Friend? Background character? Possibly smallest cock in the room?

Peter leaned against the railing beside him, silent for a few minutes. "You ever feel like you're the only one not in on the joke?"

Donald smirked. "All the time."

Peter nodded. "Good. Thought it was just me."

Four drinks in, the mood shifted.

Nia was dancing with three different strangers holding a bottle of Prosecco. Kristal had dragged Julian onto the floor to prove she had rhythm. Terry stood off to the side, sipping her drink, a soft smile on her lips as the bass throbbed.

Donald caught her eye. He didn't say anything, just gave a subtle tilt of his chin.

Terry raised an eyebrow, and he shrugged. She waded into the hum of the room, letting everyone blur as she moved toward Donald.

"You trying to dance?" she asked, loud over the music.

"With you? Always." Donald said, voice smooth and cocky.

The beat dropped, something dark and dirty and Terry moved first, rolling her hips against him with more confidence than she expected. Donald met her halfway, his hands settling low on her waist like muscle memory. The space between them disappeared.

She pressed her back into his chest, grinding slow as the bass pounded. His hands slid over her hips, gripping her, remembering every inch. When she turned to face him, his hands didn't move. Their bodies stayed locked, swaying like they were alone in the dark.

"Jesus, you smell good," he murmured. "What is that?"

"Hempz lotion and some of Kristal's perfume. And your hands are on my ass."

"Should I move them?"

"Don't you dare."

She tilted her head up, lips parted, and Donald kissed her. Right there in the middle of the dance floor. It was sloppy, urgent, hungry. She moaned softly against his mouth as his hands slid lower. Their hips stayed moving, in rhythm with the beat, with each other, with everything they thought they'd lost.

She bit his lip lightly before pulling back just enough to whisper, "We're disgusting."

"Wanna go be disgusting somewhere else?" Donald grinned.

Terry smiled, grabbed his hand without another word and pulled him off the floor. She led him through the crowd like she knew exactly where she was going. They slipped past the bar, down a short hallway, and into the dim, single-stall bathroom. She locked the door behind them with a loud click.

For a second, neither of them moved. The sound of muffled bass thumped through the walls. Her breath hitched. His chest rose and fell hard.

Then she turned, leaned back against the sink, and lifted her dress up to her waist—no hesitation, no panties.

Donald's eyes went wide.

"Holy shit."

"Yeah," she said, a little breathless. "I planned ahead."

He stepped in fast, fumbling his belt with one hand, the other already on her thigh. His pants dropped just low enough. He freed his cock, thick, already hard, and pressed her against the sink.

"You sure?" he asked, eyes scanning hers.

"Will you hurry the fuck up! I'm your wife. Of course I'm sure."

Terry reached between them, guiding him in with one slick stroke. Donald groaned deep and guttural as her heat swallowed him. His cock slid in slow, surrounded by waves of her wetness. She let out a moan and pulled him in closer.

"Fuck me. Fuck me hard."

Donald obliged. They moved fast and desperate. Her back thudded softly against the mirror with each thrust. One of his hands gripped the edge of the sink for leverage, the other snaked around to hold her neck, forehead resting against hers.

"Fuck, babe," he whispered, lips brushing her cheek. "You feel so good."

She moaned biting into his shoulder, clutching his shirt. "Don't stop. God, don't—"

He didn't.

Each thrust was harder, sloppier. The sound of him slamming in and out of her made Terry go wild. She gasped, nails digging into his back. He grabbed her thigh and lifted it higher, plunging deeper, her dress hiked up to her ribs. Their rhythm turned frantic, all teeth and breath and need.

"Don't stop, I'm about to cum," she cried as she clenched her pussy around his throbbing rod. Then she let out a moan. She was shaking and leaking down his balls. He barely lasted another pump before spraying inside her. His hips stuttering, forehead now pressed to her shoulder.

They stood there, tangled and catching their breath. Terry letting out smaller moans as his cock pulsed inside of her, releasing all of his foam.

"I should ruin your life more often," she whispered, still breathless.

He laughed into her neck. "Yeah, well... we're not done yet."

But just as quickly as they began their tryst, the moment passed.

They straightened up in silence, breathing still heavy, both staring at their reflections in the smudged mirror. Terry tugged her dress back down, smoothing it over her hips. Her cheeks were flushed, hair slightly messed. Donald tucked his softening cock away and zipped up, blinking like he'd just come out of a dream.

"You good?" she asked, fixing a curl that had slipped loose.

"Barely," he muttered. "You?"

She gave a crooked smile. "I'm walking out of here like nothing happened. Try to keep up."

They stepped out one after the other, Terry first, Donald right behind, closing the door softly like that made any difference. The music hadn't changed, the crowd still swayed, but it felt louder now. Brighter.

Julian spotted them first, drink in hand. He raised his brows as they approached. "Well damn. Y'all missed a whole set."

"Bathroom line was brutal," Terry said smoothly, brushing past him.

Julian smirked. "Mmhmm. That's why you both look like you just survived a hurricane."

Donald cleared his throat and grabbed a drink from the bar.

Kristal clocked the tension immediately, eyes darting between the two of them. She didn't say anything. Just looked slowly over the rim of her glass as she danced.

Nia danced by, looping an arm around Terry's waist. "Okay, sexy. You better glow. You need to go to the bathroom more often if it's gonna fix your whole vibe and shit."

Terry laughed, forcing coolness she didn't feel. "Just needed a minute."

Donald tried not to trip over a barstool walking to their reserved table. Kristal made her way back to the table; cheeks flushed from dancing and alcohol.

"Where's Peter been?" she asked, flopping into the booth.

"Smoking on the balcony," Nia said, licking salt off her hand from a tequila shot. "With a girl named Mackenzie who looks like she teaches hot yoga and eats men for protein."

"Wow. Specific." Kristal blinked.

"I'm gifted," Nia replied.

"To making memories." Julian raised his glass.

"To surviving them." Donald said as he raised his and smiled at Terry.

The night raged on as the group continued to have fun.

It was after 1 a.m. when the group made it back to the house. They trickled in at different paces. Donald walked in first with his hands in his pockets, facial expression not exuding any emotion. Nia and Kristal were loud and laughing; Peter and Terry talking low and close; Julian was quiet behind them all.

Terry had laughed with Peter all the way up the front steps, tossing her shoes off in the foyer like she didn't have a care in the world. She barely glanced in Donald's direction before disappearing into the living room with Nia and Kristal, voices low and playful.

Donald didn't go straight to bed when they got in the house. He stood in the kitchen for a moment, the buzz from earlier fading fast. Whatever had happened between him and Terry on the dance floor, whatever that was in the bathroom, it hadn't traveled home with them. Not really. It was like flipping a switch: one second, fire. The next, frost.

So, he poured himself a glass of water and stepped out onto the back porch. The air was crisp, clean and quiet in a way that made you think too much.

He sank down on the steps, elbows on his knees, sipping slowly.

For a few minutes, he just sat there, staring out into the darkness filled with light sounds of waves. He let his mind drift through the strange, tangled knot of the evening. His marriage. His guilt. The ache that wouldn't go away, even after sex. Especially after sex.

EPISODE: 6: A Moonlight Yes

He didn't hear the door creak open behind him. Then—clink. A glass touched down beside him, followed by the soft rustle of someone sitting close.

He turned his head and saw it was Kristal.

She took a sip of wine and looked out into the darkness with him.

"Fun night?" she asked.

"Surreal." Donald exhaled.

"Mmhmm." Kristal hummed. "Terry looked... complicated tonight."

He didn't answer.

"I mean, the way she's been laughing with Julian and Peter. Either she's over everything, or she's pretending really hard."

Still, Donald stayed quiet. The silence between them grew warm, weighted.

Kristal leaned in, shoulder just brushing his. "You know, sometimes we cling to what we had because we're scared of who we might become without it."

Donald looked at her, something shifting in his expression.

"I don't think I'm scared anymore," he said quietly.

"Good." Kristal smiled, slow and sultry.

She didn't kiss him. But she didn't need to.

Not yet.

The air between them had that impenetrable, magnetic charge. The kind that hovers when two people know exactly what they want but aren't sure if they'll survive it.

Her thigh brushed his, lightly. Just enough to say, I see you. Just enough to leave a figurative mark.

"You wanna know a secret?" she asked, voice so low it almost got lost in the hush of waves.

Donald nodded slowly. "Yeah."

Kristal played with her wine, swirling lazy circles like she was writing something invisible between them. "I thought about you. That whole trip. Even when we were... together."

His eyes lifted to hers.

"While we were all messing around?"

"Especially then." Kristal gave a smile.

Donald's pulse thrummed in his throat. He tried to say something, tried to make a joke, maybe ask her if she was drunk. But nothing came out. The light trickled off her legs like melting glass. Her robe clung to her hips, transparent in the moonlight.

"But," she added, pausing with one hand on her hip, "I'm not going to be the woman someone falls into just because she's there. I've done that already."

"You're not just here. You've been here."

She nodded once. Like she believed him, but it still wasn't enough.

"Good night, Donald."

She kissed him on the neck, stood up and left. No teasing. No games. Just the quiet, undeniable certainty of a woman who knew exactly what she deserved.

Donald didn't follow her.

He stayed on the porch, staring out at the moon's reflection slicing silver lines through the ocean. His pulse hadn't slowed. His hands felt twitchy, restless.

Kristal had lit a fuse, and now he was sitting in the afterglow with nothing to do but burn.

He rose, grabbed a towel, and disappeared inside quiet, and slow. His mind already spiraling.

The guest bathroom was cool and clean. Dimly lit. He turned on the faucet just to hear something. Just to drown out the racing thoughts.

Donald didn't undress completely, just unzipped and braced himself over the sink with one hand. His other hand found what his mind couldn't let go of–Kristal's voice. The way she said, "You touched me like I was real." Her legs glistening in the light. That robe hugging her hips.

He stroked himself slowly at first with a soft pull, jaw clenched, forehead pressed to the mirror. The rhythm built without thought. It wasn't fantasy. It was memory and he was soaked in it. His breath fastened as the dry stroke on his cock got harder. He whispered her name once hoarse, broken.

As the throbbing pulsed, he finished with a muted groan, biting down on the grunt as his whole body shuddered against the porcelain sink. His load coated the edge of the drain.

He cleaned up methodically. Like he hadn't just come to the thought of a woman he never truly got to know but couldn't stop seeing now. He splashed water on his face and stared into the mirror like it might offer him some kind of answer.

It didn't.

Kristal lay on her bed, robe half untied, one leg draped over the edge like she owned the mattress and the world it rested in. Her hair was still damp, and her skin was warm from the shower. But her mind was miles away.

She closed her eyes and let herself feel it. The frustration. The anticipation. The knowing that Donald was somewhere on the other side of the house probably just as wound up.

She slipped her hand between her thighs and gasped softly at the first touch. She looked around and didn't see Peter, so she continued the play.

Her fingers slid up and down her folds. She let the moisture build, before inserting them. She didn't go fast, didn't need to. It wasn't just about getting off; it was about claiming her power back. Reclaiming her body from memory. From old rhythms. From moments that almost happened.

She pictured Donald's mouth licking her moist hole, letting his tongue lap her up. His voice when it dropped just slightly. His hands steady, reverent.

She moaned into the pillow and let it roll through her. Slow, deliberate, soaking the sheet with the kind of heat no fan could cool.

Her body began to shudder as she climaxed, crying his name into the pillow. After, she laughed to herself. Just once. Then rolled over and stared at the ceiling, as she tasted her work with the faintest smile playing on her lips.

The house had quieted.

Terry stood at the base of the stairs, hand resting on the banister, listening to Nia and Julian still laughing softly in the living room. Their voices were loose with alcohol and comfort, ping-ponging off each other in a rhythm.

Peter had already said his goodnights, barely looking at Terry as he passed.

Typical, she had thought.

She'd offered a small wave; he didn't return it. She didn't care. Not really.

She glanced toward the front windows. Still no sign of Donald. Or Kristal. Her jaw tensed.

She turned slowly and climbed the stairs. Every step felt louder than it should've in the quiet house, her feet soft against the hardwood. The bedroom door opened with a sigh, like even the room was tired of pretending things were normal.

Terry sat on the edge of the bed but didn't move to undress. She just stared at the floor.

The night had been confusing. The sex in the bathroom had been impulsive. Filthy. Necessary. But afterward? Donald hadn't reached for her hand. Hadn't even looked at her on the ride back.

She chewed on the inside of her cheek as Donald's remnants leaked out of her. Why did it feel like she'd just scratched an itch instead of making love to her husband?

She looked to the glass door and to the open hallway door. Still no sign.

"What the fuck is he doing? What else does he want from me?"

That thought sank into her gut like a cold stone.

Terry stood, finally unzipping the green dress and letting it fall to the floor. No ceremony. No sentiment. She tossed the cum stained dress with her dirties, pulled on one of Donald's old T-shirts from her suitcase and crawled into bed. The sheets were cool, untouched. She rolled to one side, then the other, restless.

We were dancing then had some fun. It was hot. He needs to get over himself.

Terry closed her eyes and took a deep breath through her nose.

She hated how much it mattered. Because if she was being honest, really honest, part of her didn't regret what happened in that bathroom.

But a bigger part of her didn't know if it meant anything to Donald.

Peter had made his way to the rooftop bar. He sat with a glass of bourbon that had long since lost its chill. His posture was casual, but his eyes were sharp. Watching the night like it owed him something.

He had seen Terry dancing earlier. Not with him. Not for him. And it gnawed at something he didn't want to name.

Terry laughed differently now, freer. And not once during the whole trip had she looked to Peter with that glow in her eyes. Not the way she used to, especially after being one with his huge dick. Not even out of habit.

It gnawed at him.

When she had leaned in toward Donald on the dance floor, smiling that soft, private smile Peter had imagined snatching her wrist. Turning her around and reminding her who made her pussy scream best. Who still could.

He exhaled slowly and pulled out his already engorged thick slab.

His hand wrapped around the thick shaft, pulling hard and fast, like he wanted to punish the thought instead of feeding it. He poured the bourbon on his shaft to lubricate.

He didn't think of Kristal. Not once.

He thought of Terry in that backless green dress. Bent forward, mouth parted.

His climax hit in a sudden, bitter burst spurting streams of cum onto the floor. As the streamers slowed to a dribble that drained down his sack, he let out a moan.

"Fuck, that was good."

He grabbed paper towels, cleaned the evidence, zipped up, downed his glass, and let the silence do the judging.

EPISODE: 7: Old Tensions, New Pressure

The scent of bacon hit first. Not the warm, comforting kind. No, this was survival-hangover bacon. The grease was heavy and clinging to the air like a prayer for mercy.

Kristal groaned into her pillow.

Her mouth tasted like tequila and her thighs were still sensitive. She rolled over carefully, blinking at the thin streaks of morning sunlight filtering through the blinds. Somewhere down the hallway, someone sneezed. Twice.

Then came Nia's voice, laughing. "If anyone touches my eggs before I get there, I swear to God I will fight you in this bathrobe."

Kristal smiled and dragged herself upright.

The house was alive with the kind of chaos that only happened when too many people tried to function under one roof. Doors slammed. Showers ran like someone was paying to baptize the whole block. Bare feet slapped the wooden floors like a herd of caffeinated toddlers. The energy wasn't tense, just freshly scrambled. Like someone had rewired the vibe in their sleep.

Kristal pulled on her robe and opened her door quietly. The hallway was already warm with the smell of coffee and the sounds of reluctant conversation.

Peter's door was closed. He was still in bed. A large lump still under the sheets.

Terry's room door was open, and the bed was empty.

Then Kristal heard Donald's voice coming from the kitchen. It was low and calm. It had that Sunday morning-in-boxers tone. Suddenly, she felt everything from last night all over again.

Terry was barefoot in the kitchen, hair down and messy, wearing one of Donald's old T-shirts and humming to herself as she flipped pancakes.

Donald leaned against the island, quietly cutting fruit.

It would've looked domestic if not for the obvious fact that they weren't touching, weren't even facing each other fully.

"Sleep okay?" Donald asked, not looking up.

"Eventually," Terry said, voice light.

Julian came in shirtless, rubbing his eyes and sniffing. "What smells like forgiveness?"

"Me," Nia said, sliding into the room with oversized sunglasses, her robe and zero shame. "Forgiveness and hot sauce."

Kristal padded in next, catching Donald's eye for just a second. The corner of his mouth lifted, barely. But her chest still fluttered.

"Y'all are way too attractive for this hour," Nia said. "I feel like someone stuffed my head with dryer lint and remorse."

"Well, the coffee's strong," Donald offered with a laugh.

"I need it stronger," Nia replied. "Preferably injected into my bloodstream."

Peter showed up last. Buttoned up. Not talking.

He nodded at the group, muttered a "morning," and went straight for the coffee like it owed him money.

The group fell into a strange kind of rhythm, talking around each other, joking without pushing too deep.

But in the pauses is where tension thrived.

Later, after breakfast, dishes clinked in the sink and the group scattered to change, to shower, and to escape awkward silence. Kristal found herself standing on the balcony with a second cup of coffee and no plan.

Donald stepped out beside her.

He didn't say anything at first. Just sipped his juice and stared out at the horizon.

Then, quietly:

"I didn't sleep much."

"Because of the drinks or because of me?" Kristal didn't look at him.

He smirked, still watching the water. "Yes."

She leaned against the railing. "We probably shouldn't have said anything last night."

He nodded. "We didn't do anything."

"Sometimes words do more damage."

"Or more good."

Kristal looked at him. "You ever wonder if we're all just orbiting the same mess? Like... no matter how far we try to drift, we end up pulled back into it?"

Donald took a long breath. "I think we're all just pretending to be okay with things we're still pissed about."

That statement landed.

She sipped her coffee. "You think Peter's okay?"

"I think his ego took a hit. Terry's glow-up isn't making it easy."

Kristal laughed softly. "You noticed that too?"

"I'm a man. I notice when other men start sweating."

They shared a look—something unspoken but understood.

Kristal turned back toward the sea. “This house needs a damn reset button.”

Inside, Peter sat alone in his room, phone in hand, not typing anything. Just staring at Terry’s Instagram page like it might offer clarity.

There was a picture she posted from their night out. Terry and Kristal, laughing over drinks. Her head tilted back, neck arched.

Peter’s thumb hovered over the screen, then stilled.

He didn’t know what he was feeling. He just knew it didn’t feel good.

He remembered kissing that neck once.

He remembered the way she used to laugh at everything he said, back when they were all crammed into that cabin, taking turns cooking, drinking and getting in touch with something they never knew they needed.

There was never anything real between Terry and Peter, just shared nights, stolen touches, and group chaos. But still he’d had her attention once. If only for a minute because of his dick and freewheeling lifestyle. But that lifestyle was with Kristal. Now, he's in the lifestyle alone.

Now, Terry looked polished and confident in a different way than before. Like she belonged in someone else’s world. Someone better than former porn actor, Rosco Slim.

Still, when he closed his eyes, the flashes came: that green dress hugging her thighs, the way she tossed her head back when she laughed, the too-long glance she gave him after breakfast.

Peter’s jaw tightened. Not because he’d lost something—he never had her.

But because it stung to be forgotten.

That afternoon, Julian proposed a beach volleyball game—men versus women. "Let's settle these centuries of gender-based injustice once and for all."

No one took the game seriously, but everyone played like it mattered.

Sweat glistened. Skin clapped against sand. Terry dove hard enough to scrape her thigh. Kristal spiked on Peter twice and didn't apologize. Donald played with the kind of focused aggression that made Kristal's stomach flip.

They collapsed in the sand afterward, laughing and breathless.

It was the first time the group actually felt like a group again.

Almost.

The volleyball game had broken just enough ice to let the sun pour in, literally and figuratively. For a few hours, it felt like they were back in their early days. Not perfect. Not without undertones. But moving. Laughing.

Peter almost looked relaxed, sand stuck to his calves and a slice of pineapple in his hand. Though, he kept glancing at Terry like he couldn't decide if she'd smile back or slap him.

She didn't do either. She just glowed.

Donald watched her too, from across the bonfire they built at dusk, but not the way Peter did.

Peter looked at her like he missed control. Donald looked at her like there was some kind of shift—an alignment he hadn't expected. And maybe he still didn't know what to do with it.

Kristal noticed both. She sat between Nia and Julian, sipping hard seltzer and laughing loud as usual, like the fire was fueling all parts of her. She wore one of her tighter dresses: black, sleeveless, low in the back. She didn't tug it down. And every time she crossed her legs, Donald's eyes flicked toward her like muscle memory.

Terry hadn't meant to lead anyone on. That wasn't her game. But being watched by both Peter and Donald stirred something in her, something she thought she'd left back in that freezing cabin in Maine. The week when everything got blurry: the laughter, the liquor, the bodies that slipped into ones they didn't belong in, and Peter spraying his hot cum on Terry's stomach.

They had all fooled around, sure. In the dark. Half-daring. But it was always tangled up with other hands, other lips. There was never a promise. Never a claim.

And yet, that look he gave her today, like she'd taken something from him, sat heavy in her chest.

Now here they were, sitting just a few feet apart under open sky, pretending the past wasn't crawling around their ankles like vines.

Terry leaned her head against Kristal's shoulder.

"You okay?" Kristal whispered, low enough to make it private.

Terry nodded, murmuring, "This feels like the part in the horror movie where the group splits up and dies one by one."

Kristal snorted. "If I die, tell Peter he's not allowed to cry unless I haunt his shower."

"I'll etch it into your urn."

They giggled, and for a moment, it helped.

But Terry's smile faded when she saw Peter talking to Nia, gesturing with the same hand that he used to finger her, slow and deep, like he knew exactly how to unravel her.

The same hand that gripped her tits like he was staking a claim.

She looked toward Donald.

He was staring into the fire. Silent. Still.

She remembered the first time she caught Donald staring, really staring.

It was that hot tub night in Maine.

Kristal was giggling about how cold the air felt on her wet skin. Peter was fiddling with the heat lamp showcasing his thick cock, and Terry had been standing at the edge of the deck in her bright yellow bikini. Her arms crossed under her chest, pretending not to notice how Donald kept stealing glances.

But the moment that stuck in her memory wasn't Kristal's moans or the mess or even Peter's size, it was the way Donald touched her arm. It was like he was trying to hold something broken.

Now she watched him sip his beer, silent and far away across the firelight, and wondered if that night was the beginning of the end?

Or was it just the first time she realized they were both already drifting?

Kristal stood and stretched, her body long in the firelight, then headed for the cooler near the back patio. She needed a break. A breather. Maybe just the illusion of distance from the way Donald looked at her like she might be the answer to a question he didn't have the guts to ask out loud.

She bent down to grab a drink, then heard footsteps behind her.

"Was I staring too hard?" Donald's voice. Soft. A little raspy.

She didn't turn. Just cracked the can open and said, "Do you want the honest answer or the flattering one?"

"Flattering," he said.

"Then no, you were subtle. Like a wrecking ball in a library."

She turned to face him finally. He was close. Closer than he probably should've been.

But Kristal didn't move.

"Are we gonna talk about last night?" he asked.

Kristal took a sip, then wiped her mouth slowly. "I think we already said everything important."

"You said you weren't gonna be anyone's fallback."

"I meant it."

"But you also said you thought about me."

"I meant that too."

He studied her.

"I would never want you to feel like a side dish, Kristal."

She crossed her arms. "Then stop serving me up like one. Say what you want."

He hesitated.

And she stepped forward, just enough that her large tits brushed his chest. Just enough that he'd have to move or claim her.

Donald didn't move.

But he didn't kiss her either.

Not yet.

"You scare me a little," he said, his voice just above the hum of fire and wind.

Kristal took another sip and gave a soft snort. "Why? Because I'm not Terry?"

"No." He paused. "Because I want you... in a way that's not simple."

She raised the can again, watching him over the rim. "I'm not simple. And I'm not safe either."

Donald gave a faint smile. "I know. That's probably why I keep looking."

Kristal raised an eyebrow. "Then stop looking and fucking do something."

He reached up, brushing hair from her cheek, letting his fingers linger just a second longer than necessary. The touch was light, so light it made her chest tighten more than if he'd just grabbed her and kissed her.

Kristal's breath caught. Her lips parted.

Then—

"Yo!" Julian's voice carried from the bonfire. "If y'all are gonna chill by the drinks, at least bring me a beer!"

Kristal closed her eyes and shook her head, grinning despite herself.

Donald stepped back with a quiet laugh, breaking the charge between them.

"Guess we're needed," he said, reaching into the cooler.

Kristal gave a mock sigh and grabbed a second drink. "Saved by the Julian. Cockblocker of the year," she muttered.

They walked back toward the group, drinks in hand, shoulders brushing once as they moved in sync. No one said anything, but it was just enough to notice.

And Peter noticed.

He watched Kristal hand Julian his drink, then she sat further away from Donald than before.

And in that moment, he knew.

But, he didn't say a word.

Not yet.

EPISODE: 8: New Tensions, New Pressure

The fire didn't feel quite as warm anymore as the wood burned down. But the jealousy in Peter was on the rise.

Peter was already watching them when Kristal walked away and Donald had followed.

He could sense the way tension shifted. And he hated it.

Not because he still wanted Kristal. Not really. That ship had sunk after the group trip, back when she caught him texting someone else and laughed like he was predictable.

But he hated not being the gravitational center. Rosco Slim was not one to be upstaged, especially by Donald. But he was thinking of the old Donald, not the new getting his shape and confidence back man that he is now.

He hated that Donald had changed. And most of all, he hated how Terry barely looked at him.

Before, Donald had been the quiet one. The "safe" one. The one who didn't push or flirt or compete.

Now he walked like he knew women wanted him. And worse, like he might want something for himself for once.

Peter downed the last of his drink and stood, brushing off his shorts.

"Where you going?" Nia asked.

"Just stretching."

He wasn't.

He was hunting for the piece of himself he didn't recognize anymore.

Later that night, after the fire had burned out and bodies scattered into hallways and couches and quiet corners, the house slipped into that strange silence. Where the walls remembered everything and the air still smelled like salt and heat and skin.

Terry lay on her bed, eyes wide open, moonlight spilling across the sheets.

She had felt Kristal tense beside her when Donald came close.

She had felt Peter's eyes on her back when she walked away.

And in her chest, something bloomed but not quite guilt or desire.

Just this deep, aching awareness that no matter how much they all pretended, nothing was ever going to be quite the same.

Kristal walked back toward her room barefoot, her sandals dangling from her fingertips, skin still warm from where Donald had brushed against her.

That momentary brushing clung to her like a second skin.

When she closed her bedroom door, she leaned against it for a long moment. Eyes shut. Heart ticking slow.

Her mind wouldn't quiet. It wandered instead to the first time she ever noticed Donald. Not as the shy one. Not as the background friend. But as a man.

In that kitchen surrounded by pizza and attraction. She found him attractive before the changes, and now she found him irresistible. The moment she opened her warm mouth to invite his cock inside. The thought of doing it when they could've been caught, the excitement she felt from him being aroused by her body, and the feel of his cum coating her mouth.

That moment had stayed tucked away in her.

She dropped her sandals, crawled into bed, and let her fingers trace that old memory like a fresh scar.

"Yes, please touch me just like that," she moaned. The thoughts of Donald being inside her replayed in her mind.

Donald didn't go to bed right away. He wandered back into the kitchen to finish his water. He leaned on the counter, staring out the back door. The moon hung heavy, draped across the sea like a secret promise.

He remembered how Kristal looked when she challenged him earlier. That spark in her eyes. The confidence. It hadn't always been there. Or maybe he'd just never been brave enough to look directly at it before.

She was no longer the woman who waited to be invited. She made space for herself. Demanded it. And that stirred something in him.

Not just lust or admiration, but something slower, more dangerous.

He wanted to be the man she wanted on purpose, not the one she fell into by accident.

Terry wasn't asleep either. She stood on the balcony outside their room, arms folded tight, wearing one of those oversized T-shirts that always made her feel small but safe.

The ocean whispered and she let it.

She thought about Peter. About Donald. About herself.

She thought about the years she'd spent minimizing her needs, so the group stayed balanced. So no one rocked the boat.

And she realized, maybe for the first time, that she didn't owe the boat anything anymore.

She'd spent so long being the peacekeeper.

Maybe now she'd let the waves do what they wanted.

She turned, walked back inside, and shut the balcony door with a click that sounded a lot like an ending.

The next morning came bright and soon.

Peter was the first one up. He couldn't sleep.

He stood in the kitchen in grey sweats and no shirt, making scrambled eggs like it was the only thing keeping him grounded.

Donald walked in behind him, silent. They nodded at each other, but it wasn't comfortable silence.

It was silence with a pulse.

Kristal passed through next, brushing past Peter without looking at him. She went straight to the fridge, grabbed an orange, peeled it with deliberate focus.

Terry, Nia and Julian joined last, yawning and soft, like the sunrise hadn't offended them yet.

"Damn," Nia muttered, "Y'all got some unresolved tension in here. Should we light sage? Get a priest?"

"Just needs more coffee," Terry said. But her eyes flicked to Peter, then to Donald and finally Kristal.

They ate quietly with light conversation.

Every glance, every shift in posture, every delayed laugh carried history.

And everyone at the table felt it.

EPISODE: 9: No One's Innocent

They'd spent the morning tiptoeing around each other like toes avoiding broken glass. Everyone seemed to be waiting for someone else to break the tension, but no one wanted to be the one holding the broom.

Donald kept busy with a morning run, push-ups on the beach, and breakfast cleanup. Anything to distract himself from the way Kristal's eyes had flashed last night, or how Terry's distant smile at breakfast felt both comforting and deeply unfair.

By mid-afternoon, Julian had grown restless. He leaned against the kitchen island, eyes narrowed thoughtfully, tapping his fingers against the marble countertop like a nervous pianist.

"I have a proposal," he announced to the group scattered around the living room, each lost in their phones or books.

Kristal glanced up from her magazine, raising one perfectly arched brow. "It better involve alcohol or a boat."

"How about both?"

"Keep talking."

"Sunset booze cruise," Julian said, lifting his arms as if unveiling a prize. "I found a charter company. Private boat, cocktails, dinner at sea, awkward dancing optional."

Kristal immediately perked up. "I'm in. I'll even bring my awkward dance moves."

Nia peeked over the edge of her book. "As long as there's tequila and sunscreen, count me in."

Donald shrugged, mildly interested. "Sure. Why not."

Terry hesitated just a fraction too long before agreeing, and Donald noticed.

"I'll pass," Peter said finally, casual enough to sound believable.

Julian raised an eyebrow. "Seriously? It'll be fun."

Peter shook his head. "Not really feeling it."

Kristal flicked her gaze toward him, unreadable. "Suit yourself. You just going to stay here and slap it around for a bit?"

"Maybe I will," Peter replied with a scowl.

^Three hours later...^

They were boarding a sleek, white boat named Serenity Now. An ironic choice, Donald thought, considering the storm clouds of unresolved emotion they'd carried aboard.

The captain, a cheerful older man named Eddie, wore a floral shirt that could've powered its own battery, and he smiled like he genuinely enjoyed being trapped on open water with strangers.

"Welcome aboard!" Eddie boomed. "Any special occasions tonight?"

"Group therapy," Kristal deadpanned.

Eddie laughed, clearly assuming she was joking, and gestured toward the deck. "Make yourselves comfortable. Open bar's at the stern. Help yourself."

Julian immediately claimed bartender duties. Donald watched him mix drinks with the ease of someone who had spent too many nights in overpriced lounges, charming strangers with polished small talk.

Terry leaned against the railing, eyes closed, face tilted to the falling sun. She looked serene and unbothered, but Donald noticed her knuckles gripping the metal railing a bit too tight.

"Hey," he murmured, approaching slowly. "You okay?"

She opened one eye, shielding her gaze from the glare. "Yeah. Just forgot how intense group vacations could get."

Donald chuckled softly. "You'd think we'd learn."

Terry gave him a half-smile, gentle and slightly sad. "Do we ever?"

At the back of the boat, Kristal stood near Julian as he effortlessly poured tequila shots into plastic cups.

She glanced up at him. "You're suspiciously good at this."

Julian grinned broadly. "Bartended through college. I learned all sorts of skills—mixology, listening to people's problems, pretending to care."

Kristal snorted. "You should've stuck with it. The pretending-to-care part might come in handy tonight."

Julian laughed, handing her a shot. "Are things really that bad?"

She tapped her cup against his. "Not yet. But the night's young."

Meanwhile, back at the house, Peter sat on the balcony, alone with a glass of whiskey he'd poured as soon as he'd watched the boat drift into the horizon.

He didn't regret skipping the outing. He was glad to finally breathe without feeling eyes on him. But the solitude felt heavier than he expected. It pressed into his chest like an accusation.

He replayed the volleyball game they had. The way Terry had laughed, genuinely laughed, not the polite chuckle she'd given him for weeks. It had felt like being a spectator to a life he wanted to star in.

Peter rubbed his forehead, irritated.

He picked up his phone, hesitating only briefly before tapping out a message.

Peter: We okay?

He stared at the screen, waiting.

Minutes passed.

Finally, three dots flashed. Disappeared. Reappeared.

Terry: Define okay.

Peter didn't respond.

The sun dipped lower as the boat moved gently through the waves, the water catching the sky's purples and golds like spilled paint. Kristal stood next to Donald, sipping slowly from her cup.

"Regretting the trip yet?" she asked softly.

"Not yet," Donald replied. "Ask me again after another drink."

She laughed quietly. "Funny. You never really struck me as the drinking-to-forget type."

Donald glanced sideways. "What type did I strike you as?"

Kristal tilted her head, thinking. "The thoughtful type. The type who overthinks but never admits it."

"You think I overthink?"

She raised her cup in mock salute. "That's a lot of 'thinks,' but yeah. Takes one to know one."

Donald grinned slowly. He liked this version of Kristal. She was honest, quietly confident, and softer around the edges. A vast difference from the wild person he knew just a few months ago.

They stood in comfortable silence for a moment until Julian called from the bar. "Alright, y'all. Dinner's served."

They moved toward the back deck table, laden with fresh shrimp, grilled vegetables, and warm bread. Eddie had lit little tea candles along the railings, creating an atmosphere almost too romantic for a group just trying to survive the weekend.

Terry sat next to Julian, Kristal slipped in next to Donald, and Nia took the seat opposite, casting amused looks at everyone like she was placing silent bets.

"So," Nia said, spearing a shrimp, "Are we playing truth or dare later, or has this group collectively decided honesty is overrated?"

Kristal laughed softly. "Let's just stick to eating. Less casualties that way."

"Where's the fun in that?" Nia teased.

Donald raised his beer, smiling dryly. "Maybe we've had enough fun."

Nia arched a brow. "Impossible. Too much fun is impossible, Sir."

They ate, they laughed, they kept conversations surface-level. Nobody ventured into the depths of yesterday's tensions.

But beneath every smile and casual glance, they were all quietly aware of the tide rising. The undercurrent growing stronger, something nobody was innocent enough to avoid.

As dinner wound down and the sky turned from vivid gold to deep indigo, Julian rose to clear plates, his easy laughter echoing gently over the rhythmic splash of waves against the boat's hull.

"I vote for some music," he declared. "Something chill. Mood-setting."

"Mood for what?" Kristal shot him a look.

He grinned. "Honesty. Or dancing. Or both."

Nia chuckled, propping her chin in her palm. "Why do I get the feeling your idea of chill isn't exactly PG-rated?"

Julian shrugged innocently. "Who said it had to be?"

He tapped something into his phone, and a sultry R&B beat spilled softly from the Bluetooth speakers, mingling with the salt air and fading sunlight. The effect was immediately intoxicating.

Kristal glanced at Donald. He was quietly watching Terry talk animatedly with Julian, their voices low, intimate. She nudged his arm gently.

"Wanna dance?"

Donald blinked. "Seriously?"

"Not everything has to mean something deep," Kristal said, eyes sparkling playfully. "Sometimes it can just mean...dancing."

Donald set his beer down. "Alright. But fair warning, I've been known to embarrass people on dance floors."

Kristal stood, tugging his hand. "Perfect. Me too."

They moved slowly to the open area of the deck, Kristal's hand lightly resting on his shoulder, Donald's palm pressed cautiously against her lower back. The sway of the boat added a subtle rhythm to their movements, gentle yet charged.

"See?" Kristal whispered, tilting her face toward him. "You're not bad."

"You're being generous."

"Maybe," she teased, leaning in slightly. "Or maybe I like what I see."

Donald's eyes met hers, intensity softening at the edges. "You've changed since last time."

"So have you."

They moved quietly for a minute, the space between them slowly shrinking.

Meanwhile, Terry watched from across the deck, a complicated warmth curling inside her chest. Not jealousy, exactly. Just a recognition, like seeing something familiar through new eyes.

She shifted slightly in her seat, and her conversation came to a stop. Julian noticed her watching.

"You good?" he murmured.

Terry nodded slowly. "Yeah. It's just...weird seeing Donald like this. Confident. Open. It almost irritates me."

"People surprise you," Julian said quietly, following her gaze. "Sometimes in good ways."

"Maybe. I guess it is good, but I had gotten used to the old Donald. I feel like I don't know this fucking guy."

Julian turned slightly, looking directly at her. "Ever wonder if you surprised yourself, Terry?"

"What do you mean?."

"I mean, maybe you surprised yourself because you didn't want to see him change. Maybe this is who he always was, but you just...ignored it." Julian smiled, understanding lingering in his expression.

Terry didn't respond. She just looked at him with a contemplating face.

Back at the house, Peter had stopped trying to pretend he wasn't counting down until everyone returned. He'd paced, poured another whiskey, stared at his phone, watched the empty driveway from the balcony, cycling through quiet regret and restless irritation.

Eventually, unable to resist the pull of memory, he found himself standing at the door to Terry's room. It was cracked open, invitingly innocent.

He stepped inside.

The room smelled faintly of her, citrus shampoo, lavender lotion, something achingly familiar.

On the dresser lay a silver bracelet she'd worn when she was stroking his dick. He picked it up, letting the cool metal dangle from his fingers. He remembered her smile that day.

He set it down gently.

Then his eyes caught a photograph propped against the mirror—an old Polaroid from their first group trip. Kristal was laughing, Donald was blurry in the background, and Terry was leaning into Peter's chest, looking up at him like he mattered.

His jaw tightened.

Peter turned away abruptly, leaving the room with a bitterness he refused to name, closing the door firmly behind him.

The boat ride back to shore was quieter, conversations fading into comfortable quiet. Nia lounged at the stern, eyes closed, basking in the moonlight. Julian sat next to Terry, both leaning against the railing, saying little but clearly comfortable in the shared space.

Kristal sat beside Donald at the bow, knees touching lightly.

"Thanks for tonight," Donald said softly, breaking the hush.

"For dancing badly or the small talk?"

He smiled faintly. "Both. But mostly just...for seeing me."

She looked away briefly, gaze fixed on the moon's reflection rippling across the water. "You deserve to be seen, Donald. You always have."

His throat tightened slightly, emotion rising unexpectedly. "No one's ever really told me that. I mean Terry used to, but it has been a long time. Our house feels like a ghost town now."

Kristal sat quietly and let the moonlight comfort the conversation.

Once they returned, the group split off silently. Donald followed Kristal up the stairs, parting ways with a gentle, lingering glance but no touch.

He entered his room alone, shut the door softly, and lay back on the bed, staring at the ceiling, heart pulsing in his ears.

Just down the hall, Kristal stood inside her room, slowly changing out of her dress, mind swirling with the tension of possibility. She touched her lips briefly, remembering how close they'd stood, how easily she could've tilted her head upward and erased all the ambiguity.

But she hadn't. And the almost still ached sweetly, deep inside her.

Across the hall, Terry sat at the edge of her bed, mind still on Julian's words: People surprise you. Sometimes in good ways. She didn't look at Donald.

She just slipped under the covers and closed her eyes, trying not to think too much about whose name she might whisper if she finally let herself dream again.

Peter finally heard the footsteps and voices, signaling the group's return. He remained in his room, pretending to read, but his eyes stayed fixed on the door, waiting for a knock he knew wouldn't come.

He turned out the lamp eventually, darkness pressing down around him, heavy with unhappiness and something sharper, more raw—envy, longing, loss.

Tonight, Peter finally admitted to himself that maybe he wasn't angry at anyone else.

Maybe he was just angry at himself.

EPISODE: 10: Playing with Fire - Part I

Morning sunlight streamed through half-open blinds, washing the walls in stripes of soft amber. The house felt thick, heavy with humidity, unspoken truths and lingering glances.

Kristal sat alone in the kitchen, nursing a coffee that had long gone cold, gaze unfocused as she stared out at the horizon. Last night replayed vividly in her mind, the warmth of Donald's gaze meeting hers, the uncertain heat flickering in his eyes, and how close they had stood, balanced precariously on the edge of something irreversible.

Sleep evaded her half the night. She replayed the multiple kissable moments they had, his careful restraint, and the way she'd walk away from him. She wasn't naïve. She knew the stakes; understood the thin line they were tiptoeing. Afterall, Donald was still Terry's husband.

Terry was one of her best friends, and someone she would often confide in. However, this was not one of those situations. The light flirting, to giving him head in the kitchen, then finally letting him cum in her, was all part of a group activity. It was a carefree, sexually liberating, thing that just happened on the trip. It was mechanical and didn't involve emotions.

This had seemingly become an alternate reality. Kristal couldn't shake the feeling that, beneath his hesitation, something had shifted. Donald wasn't just cautious; he was afraid. Afraid of what he might lose and perhaps even more afraid of what he truly wanted.

"Good morning," Donald's voice interrupted gently from behind her.

"Oh...morning." She turned, startled, heart racing caught mid-thought.

He hesitated at the kitchen doorway, seeming uncertain whether to step fully inside. After the tense moment, he moved toward the coffee pot, pouring himself a cup in silence.

Kristal watched him closely, noting the subtle tightness in his shoulders, the careful way he evaded her eyes.

"Sleep well?" she finally asked, attempting casualness.

Donald glanced briefly at her, then back to his coffee. "Not particularly. You?"

"Not really," she admitted softly, honesty spilling out before she could reconsider. "Lots to think about, I guess."

Donald nodded slowly, his voice tight. "Same."

Before the conversation could continue or become more complex, footsteps padded down the hallway. Terry entered the kitchen, hair still tousled from sleep, eyes brightening when she saw Donald standing by the counter.

"Morning," she said warmly, stepping up to kiss his cheek softly. Donald leaned into her touch, the gesture easily natural. Kristal felt an unexpected kink in her chest.

"Good morning," Donald replied, smiling faintly.

Terry glanced toward Kristal, her expression polite yet guarded.

"Morning, Kristal."

"Morning, Terry," Kristal returned evenly, her gaze steady but neutral. The air between them rippled subtly; understanding, curiosity, maybe even suspicion, but neither woman said anything.

“Have you seen Peter?” Terry asked lightly, stepping toward the fridge. “He skipped the boat ride last night and was locked up in his room when we got back. I hope he’s okay.”

“I haven’t,” Kristal replied. “I assumed he needed some space. All of us being together again since...well you know, it might be a little weird for him.”

"Hmm. Why would it be? I mean you two are cordial, scratching the surface of friendship." Donald asked.

"He can be self-centered and since he is not my center anymore, he can be weird sometimes. We went out for coffee one afternoon, and you would think we were two Tinder strangers, just hoping the other one wasn’t a murder."

Terry paused briefly, her voice dropping slightly. “He’s a nice guy, but he always needed a lot of space.”

Kristal nodded quietly, understanding the implication all too well. The silence that followed felt weighted with complicated emotions.

Upstairs, Peter was awake, but he wasn’t ready to face the day.

He lay in bed, eyes fixed on the ceiling, thoughts looping relentlessly. The empty house had left him too much time to think, too much space to reflect on how everything had changed.

He’d always prided himself on emotional control, on being detached enough to manage relationships without complications. But now, that carefully constructed façade felt dangerously thin. He’d found himself replaying conversations, analyzing glances, regretting choices. For the first time, he wondered if detachment hadn’t been his strength at all but instead his weakness.

He knew he couldn't avoid the group forever, yet he felt oddly paralyzed. Facing Terry again meant confronting not just his lingering desire, but also the undeniable reality that Donald was more present now, more confident, more desirable, even to Terry.

With a heavy sigh, Peter finally swung his legs over the bed, forcing himself upright. Avoidance had never been his style, and he wouldn't let it start now.

By noon, everyone had gathered on the rooftop, lounging on chairs, sipping cold drinks, and pretending the night before had been nothing more than harmless fun.

Nia lay on her back, sunglasses perched on her nose, sun-warmed skin glowing. She watched the group silently for several minutes before suddenly speaking up, voice playfully challenging.

"Is it just me, or is this trip turning into one long, extremely awkward first date?"

Julian laughed from across the deck. "Depends, are we counting the boat ride as a second date, or is that still first-date territory?"

Kristal cracked a faint smile. "I'd say it's complicated enough for third-date anxiety at least."

Peter finally appeared, stepping onto the deck with careful indifference, sunglasses hiding whatever expression lingered behind them. He nodded briefly, "Morning, everyone."

Nia lowered her glasses just enough to look at him.

"Welcome back to the land of the living, stranger. Missed you last night."

"Did you?" Peter replied smoothly, feigning a relaxed smile. "Seems like everyone managed fine without me."

"We are all a team, and we were missing an important player," Terry shot out.

Donald tensed slightly but said nothing.

Peter chuckled, "Well, I did score three touchdowns in one game before."

"See, very important player," Terry replied raising her mimosa.

Julian, sensing the rising pressure, stood up abruptly. “Alright, clearly we need a distraction. Anyone up for a game of Truth or Dare? Maybe actually get some honesty flowing for once.”

“Damn, you’re brave,” Nia remarked dryly.

“Or just foolish,” Kristal added, glancing subtly toward Donald. She wondered if he’d meet her look; he didn’t.

Julian shrugged, undeterred. “Either way, it beats awkward silences.”

Peter raised an eyebrow. “Or creates new ones.”

“Even better, friends can have some silence once in a while,” Julian said confidently. “Who’s in?”

Nia sat up, “I’ll bite. Might as well embrace the mess we’re playing in.”

“Fine. I’m in.” Kristal sighed, pretending reluctance.

“Me too.” Terry hesitated.

Peter’s mouth twitched slightly. “I’m game.”

They all looked at Donald expectantly.

“Alright,” he said softly. “Let’s do it.”

The group circled up near the pool, drinks in hand, expressions cautiously guarded. Julian spun an empty beer bottle theatrically in the center of their circle.

It landed on Kristal first. Julian grinned mischievously.

"Truth or dare, Kristal?"

"Truth."

Julian leaned forward slightly, eyes glittering playfully. "Who here surprised you most on this trip?"

Kristal paused. The group watched intently. She swallowed, deciding honesty was safer than lies. "Donald."

Everyone's eyes moved quickly to Donald, whose face flushed slightly, eyes fixed on the ground.

"Interesting," Julian murmured, clearly enjoying himself. "Your turn, Kristal."

Kristal spun, the bottle pointed directly at Terry. Their eyes met, brief, cautious, complicated.

"Truth or dare, Terry?" Kristal asked softly.

Terry exhaled slowly, choosing carefully. "Truth."

Kristal's eyes narrowed slightly, tone gentle but pointed. "Are you happy, Terry? Really happy?"

The group went silent, breaths held quietly. Terry hesitated, and looked to Donald, then to Peter, before finally settling somewhere distant.

"I'm trying to be," she finally whispered. "Isn't that enough?"

Donald's heart twisted uncomfortably at her words. He didn't say anything, just looked at her and nodded.

Peter quietly sipped his drink, eyes hidden behind dark lenses.

Julian smiled faintly, breaking the nervous silence. "Well... shit."

Nia laughed softly. "Told you this was gonna get messy."

Terry cleared her throat theatrically, spinning the bottle. This time, it landed on Peter. A small smile curved Kristal's lips.

"Truth or dare, Peter?"

Peter adjusted his sunglasses, feigning indifference. "Dare."

Terry grinned wickedly, clearly enjoying the chance to provoke. "Alright, I dare you to kiss the person you've thought about the most on this trip. And it can't be the mirror."

"Oh, damn, she didn't have to do you like that," Julian said with a laugh.

Everyone chuckled at the jab. Peter cleared his throat briefly.

Slowly, he stood, moving deliberately toward Terry. Donald tensed instinctively, fingers tightening around his glass. Kristal shifted uneasily.

Peter paused in front of Terry, leaned down, and brushed a gentle, lingering kiss on her cheek. It was soft enough to be innocent, but prolonged enough to whisper unspoken words. Terry's eyes fluttered shut momentarily, lips parting slightly in surprise, or maybe something else.

Donald felt his stomach knot, jealousy sparking sharply inside him. He forced himself to breathe evenly, swallowing down emotions he wasn't ready to challenge.

Peter stepped back, returning to his seat without a word. Terry's cheeks got warm, her fingers nervously traced patterns on her thigh. Julian nodded appreciatively, breaking the dense stillness again.

"Alrighty then, Peter...your turn."

Peter spun the bottle quickly, barely glancing as it landed on Donald. Everyone stilled, awaiting Peter's choice.

"Truth or dare, dude?" Peter's voice was calm, unreadable.

"Truth," Donald replied quicker than Terry expected.

Peter's lips twitched faintly, eyes coolly analytical.

"What's your biggest regret right now?"

Donald swallowed tightly. Kristal's presence next to him felt suddenly too warm, too charged. He forced himself not to look directly at her. Instead, his eyes drifted toward Terry, seeing her uncertainty, her quiet vulnerability.

"My biggest regret," he began soft but firm, "is not always knowing how to express what I really feel. I regret letting things stay unsaid when they should've been spoken."

The group remained quiet, absorbing his words. Terry's expression softened, eyes shimmering with quiet acknowledgment. Kristal felt an uncomfortable pang of disappointment mixed with admiration for respecting his honesty. But, she was acutely aware of what he wasn't saying directly.

"Wow, powerful stuff, man." Julian said looking to Nia, who smirked playfully.

"Dare," she said immediately, crossing her legs confidently.

Julian chuckled, clearly grateful for her bravado.

"I dare you to jump into the pool fully clothed."

Nia laughed, pushing herself up without hesitation. "Easy enough. Watch and learn."

Everyone laughed softly as Nia theatrically jumped into the pool, splashing loudly, breaking the tension momentarily. She surfaced, pushing wet hair out of her face, laughing brightly.

"You're welcome," she called out, swimming leisurely. "Bomb officially diffused. For now."

"Hey, what about you?" Donald asked Julian.

"Who me? I'd take a little of both. Truth is, I love this trip. It's been a little weird, sure. But I have had fun with you guys."

Nia called from the water, "Dare you to jump in the pool naked."

Everyone got quiet.

"Naked huh? Well, see the thing is..."

"Quit thinking of an excuse and jump, dude," Peter called from the side. "Most of us have seen each other naked anyway."

"Uhh, sure. Fuck it!" Julian yelled as he snatched off his board shorts and shirt. His flaccid cock fluttered free from the confines of his shorts. Then he jumped into the pool.

Nia, Terry and Kristal stared as his cock flapped with the jump. His freshly waxed crotch meant no angle of view was blocked. His large bulbous cock head sat upon a soft but thick shaft.

"Damn, nice meat you got there," Nia said with a laugh.

"You know, I do what I can. But make sure you use your imagination. This water can do some things to it," Julian laughed.

Nia kept her bottoms but slid off her top. Her tits floated just under the water. The right one was slightly smaller than the left, but they looked great.

"We doing this again?" Donald asked, looking at Peter.

"I'm not. Just watching some friends have fun."

"Shit, I'm up for it," Terry said standing up.

She took her top off freeing her round full tits. She hopped in the pool with a large splash. The spontaneous action caught Donald off guard. He wasn't sure if he was ready for more group activity.

"I forgot how amazing your rack was, Terry." Julian said as she jumped in. Donald shot him a look. "Just fucking with you dude. I've never seen more than work cleavage."

"Ohh, ha ha. That's funny." Donald replied dryly.

Nia, Terry and Julian played in the pool as the others drank and watched. The afternoon waned, the group gradually dispersed, conversations growing quieter, introspective.

EPISODE: 11: Playing with Fire - Part II

Terry, with her top back on, lingered near the poolside, idly swirling the last of her drink, lost in thought.

Peter approached her carefully, stopping a respectful distance away.

"Mind if I join you?" he asked quietly.

"Not at all."

He sat beside her, hush falling briefly. Finally, Peter spoke, voice low and genuine. "I meant what I said, or rather, what I showed you. You've been on my mind a lot this trip."

"Peter, we had a moment back then, but it would never work. We'd just ended up hurting each other."

"I know," he admitted softly, gaze fixed on the water. "But maybe...I don't know. Maybe it's different now. Or maybe I've changed."

She glanced at him, expression cautious. "People don't change overnight."

"Maybe not," he said carefully, "but sometimes we finally see things clearly."

"You were just with Kristal. She's...my best friend and I can't have an actual relationship with you. What we did, all together was--magical. But that's over now."

Peter nodded quietly, not pushing further. For now, just sitting quietly felt like enough.

Inside, Kristal stood at the kitchen island, pouring another glass of wine, feeling strangely adrift. She heard footsteps behind her, instantly recognizing Donald's quiet approach.

"You okay?" he asked gently, standing beside her, careful not to touch her.

"Sure," she lied, offering a half-hearted smile. "Just processing everything."

Donald's words were slow, carefully chosen. "About what I said at the game? I meant it. I really struggle to say what I feel. But...I want you to know, whatever...this thing is between us, it's not something I take lightly."

Kristal looked up sharply, eyes serious. "Neither do I. And honestly, that scares me. I don't want to hurt Terry or you."

"I know," he admitted softly. "Neither do I. But pretending like I don't feel something would be a lie."

"So, what do we do?" Kristal exhaled slowly.

Donald looked squarely, the honesty between them almost painful. "I don't know yet. Maybe nothing. Maybe something. But I think, whatever it is, it has to happen carefully."

Kristal nodded slowly, quietly agreeing even as her heart ached slightly. "Carefully," she repeated softly, as if tasting the word. "I think I can manage carefully."

"Good. Good." Donald repeated as he turned and walked into the living room.

Later that evening, Julian found Nia lounging alone on the back patio, sipping leisurely from a glass of chilled rosé. He sat beside her, stretching out comfortably.

"Thanks for being the tension-breaker today," Julian said grinning softly. "You've got quite the gifts on you."

Nia chuckled, eyes sparkling playfully. "Someone had to do it. Everyone was wound tighter than piano strings. Besides, you brough a package yourself."

“Can’t argue that,” Julian admitted, shaking his head slightly. “Still, you seemed to navigate it pretty easily.”

“Life’s too short for unnecessary drama,” Nia replied lightly. “Besides, this group’s drama might be messy but it’s also fascinating as hell. I think the dynamics can withstand things others wouldn’t.”

“Fair point. Any predictions how it'll all end?”

She tilted her head thoughtfully, studying him with gentle amusement. “Not sure yet. But something tells me it’s far from settled.”

“Probably right,” Julian agreed, leaning back comfortably. “Just glad to have someone else watching from the sidelines.”

"Oh, sweetheart none of us are on the sidelines. Not really.”

Julian raised an eyebrow, intrigued by the statement. “You trying to have a private naked session or something?”

"Oh my God. Shut up Jules. No, you're not jabbing me with that thing."

"Hey, everyone needs a good dick down sometimes."

Nia just shook her head and laughed.

As the night fell deeper, Donald stood quietly on the balcony, looking out over the moonlit ocean. The waves crashed softly, a rhythmic reminder of how easily tides shifted, pulling you in directions you didn’t always understand or expect.

Terry approached softly, wrapping her arms gently around him from behind, cheek resting lightly on his shoulder.

“Long fucking day, huh,” she murmured quietly.

Donald nodded slowly, turning slightly to face her. “Yeah. Shit was complicated, too.”

Terry grabbed Donald's face and looked deeply in his eyes.

"Are we okay, Donald? Really?"

The weight of her question was heavy on his heart. Slowly, he spoke, words honest and vulnerable.

"I want us to be. I think we can be."

She studied him silently, absorbing his sincerity, feeling the quiet hope woven into his words. Her thumb traced tenderly against his jaw.

"Then let's try," she whispered. "Let's really try."

Donald nodded, leaning into her touch, feeling a quiet reassurance in her warmth. But even as he held her, something uneasy lingered inside him; a shadow of doubt, desire, and fear that refused to fully fade. Because he knew deep down, no matter how hard they tried, something had already changed.

The house felt charged, as if everyone had awakened sensing the fragile thread connecting them was finally ready to snap.

Morning brought an uneasy quiet, each person carefully tiptoeing around the others, cautious of saying the wrong thing.

Kristal stood at the kitchen counter, slicing fruit with forced nonchalance, her movements precise, controlled. Donald hovered nearby quietly fixing coffee, occasionally looking toward her. But he never lingered too long. Terry sat at the kitchen table by Nia, scrolling silently through her phone, her expression distant.

Peter appeared in the doorway last, eyes shadowed, shoulders tense.

"Morning," he greeted the room with a friendly voice that betrayed his face.

A chorus of subdued replies echoed softly back at him.

Peter poured himself coffee, pausing only briefly to glimpse toward Terry. She didn't look up. Instead, her attention remained firmly on her phone, but the deep sigh displayed her awareness of him.

Donald watched their silent exchange. A slight flair of irritation and jealousy unexpectedly filled his heart. He knew that their marriage was in trouble, but he was not going to standby why Peter ogled his wife.

As thoughts of protection ran through Donald's mind, he felt Kristal's eyes on him. He deliberately looked away, not ready to navigate those turbulent waters this morning.

Julian stepped into the kitchen, immediately sensing the charged atmosphere. He frowned lightly, scanning everyone's tense posture and carefully blank faces.

"Damn, did I walk into a funeral, or are we all just secretly plotting murder?" he joked, trying to lighten the mood.

"A little bit of both." Nia snorted softly.

"Great. Guess I'll go hide the knives." Julian shrugged.

"Probably wise." Kristal forced a smile, grateful for his attempt at humor.

After breakfast, Terry slipped outside, needing air and distance. The patio was still, the ocean stretching out ahead like a flat pulse, calming but not enough to silence the swirl in her chest. She wrapped her arms around herself and walked toward the water, barefoot on the wooden planks.

The sliding door opened behind her.

She didn't need to look to know who it was.

Peter's steps were slower than usual. Measured. Hesitant.

"Can we talk?" he asked, voice stripped of its usual bravado.

Terry sighed. "Peter, I really don't think now's a good time."

"Come on," he said, stopping a few feet behind her. "We've been dancing around it since we got here."

She turned, arms still folded, her face filled with annoyance. "Dancing around what, exactly?"

"You know what," he said. "That night back in Maine. It wasn't just some freaky group shit. You felt it too. You still feel it."

Terry blinked at him, stunned for a second before she laughed, short and humorless. "Are you serious right now?"

Peter stepped forward. "You can lie to them, but don't lie to me."

"You think one night of wild, drunken sex means we had something?" she said, incredulous. "Peter, I had your dick in me for ten minutes, not your heart."

He flinched, but she didn't stop.

"You were my best friend's boyfriend. And we were all doing something stupid, messy, and impulsive. That was it. A vacation fantasy."

"Yeah, maybe. But I saw the way you looked at me. Hell, I see it now."

"You don't see anything," she snapped. "You're mistaking regret for chemistry. We got drunk, we got naked, and then we went home. I'm not pining for round two, and I'm not looking for validation from a B-rated porn actor. Okay, Rosco?"

Peter swallowed hard, trying to hold on to his confidence, but it was slipping fast.

"So, you're just gonna act like none of it mattered?"

"It didn't matter the way you wanted it to." Her voice softened but lost none of its clarity. "I'm trying to work on my marriage, Peter. You? You're just trying to win at something because for the first time, you're not the one being chased."

Peter's face hardened, his tone turning defensive. "You really think Donald's all in? You haven't noticed how cozy he's gotten with Kristal lately?"

Terry's jaw clenched. "You don't get to bring up my husband. Not when you're the one sniffing around someone else's wife like a damn stray."

Peter's expression cracked, just for a second, into something closer to shame. He looked away.

She stepped forward. "We made a mess back then. But this? This right now? I'm not making it worse just to stroke your ego."

He opened his mouth, maybe to fight back, maybe to apologize, but she turned before he could say anything.

"You should go back inside," she said over her shoulder. "Before you say something else you'll regret." Then continued walking.

Peter stayed behind, fists in his pockets, the ocean breeze doing nothing to cool the heat rising in his chest.

Inside the house, Donald moved restlessly from room to room, feeling increasingly trapped by the unspoken words suspended between everyone. Eventually, he found himself alone in the den, pacing slowly as he tried to clear his head.

Kristal found him there a few minutes later, standing silently in the doorway, uncertain if she should interrupt. Donald turned at her soft footsteps, meeting her with conflicted eyes.

"You okay?" she asked quietly, stepping closer.

"Not even close," he admitted softly, rubbing his forehead wearily. "Everything feels like it's spiraling. I don't even know how we got here."

Kristal watched him closely, heart aching at the obvious strain etched into his features. "Maybe because none of us have been truthful, not fully."

Donald exhaled heavily, frustration mingling with resignation. "Maybe."

She stepped closer, her voice dropping even lower. "You can talk to me, you know. Honestly."

He hesitated. "Kristal, I don't think I can handle honesty right now. Especially not with you."

"Why?" she pressed gently. "Because you know how you feel?"

"Because it scares me," he admitted softly, meeting her eyes directly. "Because once we say certain things, we can't take them back."

Her breath hitched slightly, understanding dawning sharply. "Donald—"

The sound of approaching footsteps broke the moment. They both swiftly stepped apart as Terry entered the den, immediately sensing the anxiety lingering between them. She looked sharply from Donald to Kristal, wariness clouding her expression.

"What's going on?" she asked cautiously, a hint of fear in her voice.

"Nothing," Donald quickly replied, forcing a casual smile. "Just talking."

"It didn't look like nothing." Terry studied them carefully, clearly unconvinced.

Kristal stepped forward calmly. “Terry, I was just checking on Donald. It’s been a stressful few days for everyone.”

“Right.” Terry nodded slowly, but her eyes remained wary.

Kristal glanced briefly toward Donald, silently communicating her regret before slipping from the room.

Donald turned to Terry, attempting a reassuring smile. “Everything’s okay.”

“Is it?” Terry’s look remained searching, uncertain.

“Of course,” he lied, reaching for her hand. She allowed him to take it, but the stiffness in her grip betrayed lingering doubts.

“I want to believe you,” she whispered softly, eyes pleading. “But right now, everything feels wrong. Off.”

“I promise, honey. She was just checking on me. I came in here to clear my head, and I guess she saw me pacing.”

"Well, okay. I guess that makes sense." She nodded slowly, desperately wanting to believe him. But deep down, she felt the subtle shift that had already taken hold. Something had irrevocably changed.

As evening approached, the group gathered outside by the fire pit, hoping to diffuse everything through forced camaraderie. But the tone still hummed with resentments and wary glances.

Julian attempted humor again, determinedly optimistic. “Okay, how about we set ground rules tonight? No drama, no tears, and definitely no passive-aggressive comments.”

Kristal laughed, raising her drink ironically. “Then we’ll all have to take vows of silence.”

Terry forced a small smile. “Might not be a bad idea.”

Peter sat silently, staring into the fire, distant and unreadable. Terry sat beside Donald, close enough to appear united but still too far for genuine comfort.

Donald felt Kristal's occasional glances like tiny electric shocks. He kept his eyes on the flames, painfully aware of the growing pressure.

Something had to give.

EPISODE: 12: Playing with Fire - Part III

Eventually, Peter's voice broke the silence, abrupt and sharp.

"I have something to say," he announced suddenly, drawing everyone's startled attention. "Something we should've talked about a long time ago."

Every pair of eyes turned to him.

Peter looked directly at Donald, his voice steady yet quietly dangerous.

"Why don't we finally clear the air, Donald? About you and Kristal. Let's stop pretending nothing's happening."

Peter's accusation hung in the air, immediate and inescapable. Every sound around them seemed suddenly amplified, the crackle of the fire, waves lapping at the shore, their collective breathing becoming shallow, unsure.

Donald stiffened, eyes narrowing, a mix of anger, shock, and defensiveness coursing through him. He felt Terry's hand tense sharply in his, but neither pulled away yet.

Kristal's face drained of color, her heart pounding frantically. She opened her mouth, searching desperately for words, but Peter's voice sliced through again, cold and unforgiving.

"Are you really going to deny it, dude?" Peter pressed relentlessly, eyes flashing with resentment. "Everyone can see it. The way you two look at each other. Pretending nothing's happening doesn't fool anyone. Might as well go ahead and admit it."

Donald stood abruptly, frustration and anger overtaking caution.

“Yo fuck you, Peter. You have no idea what you're talking about.”

“Don’t I? You think I’m blind? Or stupid?”

"I vote for stupid," Kristal interjected, but no one reacted to her statement.

Julian raised his hands, attempting to mediate.

“Guys, guys maybe we should all calm—”

“No,” Terry interrupted, standing, her voice shaking slightly. “Let him finish.”

She turned slowly toward Donald, arms folding to her chest. “Is it true? Is something happening between you and Kristal? Is that what I saw?”

Donald hesitated, chest tight, panic flickering in his eyes. “Terry—”

“Yes or no, Donald?” Terry demanded softly, voice trembling but determined. “I want the truth. I need the truth. We can't work on a damn thing if it's covered in lies and horse shit.”

Donald felt Kristal’s desperate, pleading eyes on him, felt Peter’s challenging stare, Terry’s heartbreaking vulnerability, and he knew lying wasn’t an option.

“Nothing is going on between us. Nothing has happened,” he said finally, voice low and firm. “I mean...not physically anyway.”

Terry’s mouth dropped, eyes glittering with unshed tears.

“Not physically. Not physically," she repeated. "But emotionally? You feel something for her, don’t you?”

Donald exhaled sharply, anguish twisting his features. "Terry, I—"

"Just answer the fucking question, please." She whispered through gritted teeth.

"Yes, okay. Yes." he finally admitted, voice cracking slightly. "I'm sorry. I never acted on anything, and..."

Terry stepped back quickly, avoiding his hand like it was a live fire.

"Don't."

Julian and Nia exchanged worried glances, silent observers to the emotional wreckage unfolding. They knew the dynamic felt weird, but had no idea that things were turning serious. They, along with Kristal, were the fun-loving spark in the group.

Kristal spoke softly.

"Terry, nothing happened. We just like talking to each other is all. It's nothing serious."

Terry turned toward her sharply, eyes blazing with betrayal and anger.

"You don't get to talk to me about this, Kristal. Not right now."

Kristal swallowed hard, tears springing to her eyes. "I swear to you—"

"Oh, I believe you haven't crossed that line yet," Terry cut her off sharply. "But you wanted to. Both of you did. That's worse than if you were fucking. At least then it's something physical and emotionless or something."

"Terry I know this seems bad, but please—" Donald's head dropped, shame thickening in his throat.

"Please what?" Terry demanded, tears finally spilling over. "Pretend like it doesn't matter? Like I haven't spent every day fighting to believe we could still make this work? I mean hell, I'm out here avoiding hearts and dick because I thought we could make it work."

Peter watched silently, his drunken satisfaction melting quickly into quiet remorse as Terry's pain echoed sharply around them. He'd wanted honesty, but seeing Terry wounded hadn't been part of his plan.

Julian rose quietly, stepping closer to Terry. "Maybe we should step inside, talk this through calmly."

"No," Terry shook her head firmly, wiping angrily at her tears. "I don't want calm. I want reality, finally. Since we're here, let's get it all out. Like a festering wound, gotta clean that shit out for it heal, right?"

She looked to Donald and Kristal again; pain etched deeply into her features.

"How long?"

"There's no...I mean it doesn't matter how long." Donald hesitated, voice barely audible.

"It matters to me!" Terry shouted suddenly, raw hurt coloring her words. "God, Donald, how long have you been lying to me?"

He flinched at her anger. "I haven't been lying—"

"Bullshit!" she shot back harshly, trembling visibly. "Every smile, every touch, every promise we've made, how many were real?"

"All of them," Donald replied hoarsely, stepping toward her desperately. "Terry, I love you. I never stopped."

"I believe that, but you started loving her too," Terry whispered bitterly. "That's the part I can't forgive."

Silence stretched painfully between them, heavy and final.

Peter shifted uneasily. "Terry, I didn't mean to--"

She turned to him sharply, eyes cold. "You knew exactly what you were doing, Peter. Don't pretend like you didn't. And Kristal was wrong, you're not stupid, you're a giant man child that wants everyone to want him. A big dick and even bigger ego does not make you the best thing ever. It just means you're sad and shallow."

Peter fell silent, chastened.

Kristal finally stepped forward again, voice steady.

"I'm sorry, Terry. For all of this."

Terry stared at her silently, sadness and anger warring visibly on her face. "I trusted you, Kristal. You were my best friend. I let you into my life, my marriage. How could you? Why couldn't you just fuck him in the bathroom and call it good. Why did you have to take his heart?"

Kristal's throat tightened painfully, tears streaming openly.

"I didn't want this, Terry. None of us did. Please believe that. I just...I don't know. When I got to know him better, I just wanted to know more."

Terry shook her head, stepping back from everyone. "I can't do this anymore."

She turned abruptly, walking swiftly toward the house, leaving painful silence in her wake.

Donald moved to follow, but Nia blocked him gently, shaking her head softly.

"Give her space, Donald. Let her process." Then she ran to catch up to Terry.

Donald's shoulders slumped heavily, defeat etched deeply into his posture.

Peter watched silently, finally speaking.

"This wasn't supposed to happen like this."

Julian shot him a sharp look, tone quiet but cutting. "What exactly did you think was going to happen, Peter? Fuck man. You wanted a reaction. Well, you got one."

Peter remained silent, guilt clear in his face, realizing too late the depth of his decision.

Donald and Kristal sat across from each other, staring into the fire pit, silent.

Terry locked herself in the bedroom, tears flowing unchecked as sobs shook her body. Betrayal and hurt consumed her, the actuality of everything finally confirmed. She felt shattered, utterly lost in the wake of truths she'd been terrified to acknowledge.

A gentle knock sounded quietly at the door. She ignored it at first, unable to face anyone yet.

"Terry, it's me," Nia's gentle voice filtered softly through the door. "Please, let me in."

After a hesitant moment, Terry unlocked the door, allowing Nia to slip inside, quietly closing it behind her.

Nia stepped forward, pulling Terry into a fierce embrace, holding her tightly as fresh sobs overtook her.

"I'm so sorry," Nia whispered gently, stroking Terry's hair soothingly. "I'm here."

Terry clung to her friend, pain pouring from her in raw waves.

"I don't know what to do, Nia. It hurts so much. I mean having problems is one thing, but I never thought about us ending. Especially like this."

"I know," Nia murmured softly, holding her tighter. "You don't have to know right now. Just let yourself feel it."

"I mean, I already felt like shit because deep down I hated the confidence Donald was getting with changing himself. Maybe, I saw this coming or something."

"Well, even if you saw something, I doubt you expected this. And not from Kristal of all people."

Downstairs, Donald now stood alone by the fire, heart heavy, eyes fixed blankly on the flames. Kristal stood up and approached cautiously.

"Donald," she whispered.

He turned slowly toward her, expression weary, heartbroken.

"Kristal, I can't."

"I know," she interrupted softly, stepping closer. "I just...I never meant for it to happen like this."

"I know," he admitted quietly. "Neither did I. But it did. Fucking drunk ass Peter."

Kristal nodded, "Yeah he had no right to do that."

Donald didn't respond.

"I'll leave you alone." She said understanding his unspoken body language.

As she turned away, Donald felt an aching void open inside him. It was loss, regret, and lingering desire mingling painfully within.

Peter sat alone on the beach late into the night, the darkness surrounding him oppressive and heavy. He told himself honesty would bring clarity, resolution. But he knew that wasn't the only reason. He thought if he could force Terry away from Donald, she would come to him. Instead, he'd only caused pain.

Footsteps thudded behind him. Julian sat beside him, staring silently out at the ocean for several long moments before finally speaking.

"Hey man, you alright?"

Peter exhaled. "Nope. Not even a little."

Julian nodded quietly.

"You hurt a lot of people tonight, Peter. Especially Terry. Did you do it for her or did you do it for yourself?"

Peter's shoulders sagged heavily.

"I don't know. God, Julian, that's the last thing I wanted. I was just drunk and mixing up feelings, I guess."

"I'm just getting to know you, but I believe you," Julian said frankly. "But intentions don't erase consequences. Somebody might not have intended to hit an old lady, but they ran the red light. Same shit."

Peter nodded, absorbing his words.

"You think they'll forgive me?"

Julian considered carefully before replying. "Maybe. But right now, I think they all hate you. Nia included."

Peter stared silently out at the dark waves, recognizing the truth in Julian's words.

"What about you? You hate me too?"

"Nah man. I think I'm far enough away to not have that visceral reaction. I am disappointed that you did this to them on what was supposed to be a fun trip. Maybe they are attracted to each other, but damn man."

"Hmm," was all Peter responded with.

Inside, Donald sat quietly at the kitchen table, head bowed. He felt utterly alone, uncertain about his marriage, guilty about Kristal, angry at Peter, and profoundly disappointed in himself.

The house felt emptier, colder, haunted by lingering echoes of the confrontation. He'd reached his breaking point, and now, he had no idea where to go from here.

EPISODE: 13: Picking Up the Pieces

The bedroom door slammed shut behind Donald with enough force to shake the frame. Terry's eyes blazed with raw, anger as she stared Donald down, her breath rapid and ragged.

"You fucking asshole," she hissed, stepping toward him, voice trembling. "How dare you? Kristal of all people?"

"Terry, please—"

"No," she snapped sharply, cutting him off. "Don't you fucking dare 'Terry, please' me. You think a bullshit apology is going to erase what you two said? How you made me feel in front of everyone?"

"It wasn't supposed to, I mean I didn't think it would happen like that," Donald growled defensively. "Peter forced my hand."

"Bullshit!" Terry shot back, turning her back to Donald as she held her head in disbelief. "You don't get to blame Peter for this, Donald. You made me look stupid. You both did. It's like I didn't even fucking matter."

"You think I planned this?" Donald retorted bitterly. "You think I wanted everyone to know that I'm fucked up enough to feel something for another woman? Your friend, our friend?"

Terry's eyes narrowed. "I don't know, Donald. Maybe you wanted a reason to finally leave. Maybe you got tired of all the hard work, got tired of me. Is this your way out? You couldn't just say you wanted to leave?"

Donald's jaw tightened, eyes blazing. "Don't you dare fucking say that. I've fought to keep this marriage together, even when it felt like you didn't give a shit."

Terry laughed bitterly. "I didn't give a shit? I've bent over backwards for this marriage, trying to keep you satisfied. But you always needed something else, didn't you?"

He grabbed her wrists roughly, emotion surging. "Maybe because you stopped looking at me like I mattered years ago. I tried so many times to make this marriage special. I treated you so well, and you just took me for granted. I think you're more pissed because someone else could find happiness being with me."

"Fuck you," she whispered furiously, yanking free and pushing him hard against the wall. Their breathing was ragged, tense, and their eyes locked on to each other.

Suddenly, Terry's mouth crashed into Donald's, all fury and fire. Their teeth clashed, tongues battling like neither of them wanted to give up ground. It wasn't tender and heartfelt. It was a challenge. A dare.

Donald grabbed a fistful of Terry's dress as she yanked at his belt, both of them pulling like they were trying to win a fight, not get undressed. She shoved his shorts and boxers just low enough to free his cock; already thick and hard she palmed it hard.

"You wanna be wanted?" she growled, breath hot against his jaw. "Then fucking show me."

"I'll show you. Bend your ass over," he replied as he took her panties off.

He flipped her onto the bed, facedown. Her dress hiked up, thighs spread wide as he positioned behind her. Donald leaned down and took a deep whiff of Terry's pussy. The smell of her scent mixed with just a little sweat drove his senses wild.

Donald plowed his face into her musky creases. His tongue found its way around her folds and already watering center. Terry moaned in pleasure as he continued to lick and suck her clit into oblivion.

Terry called out, "Put it in. I want it in me now."

Donald sat up and wiped his mouth with the back of his hand. With slick heat and attitude, Terry gripped his shaft, lined him up, and he plunged in. There was no teasing, no buildup, just raw need and wet heat. Her head popped back with a sharp gasp as he grabbed her hair with his thrust.

"You like when I treat you like this, Terry," Donald hissed, pulling hard on her hair and smacking her ass with the other hand, hard enough to bruise.

"Yes! Treat me like shit. Don't stop baby," she cried out.

Their moans and continuous dirty talk filled the now musky room.

"Tell me," she demanded breathlessly. "Tell me you fucking want me, Donald. That you still need me."

"I fucking want you," he growled, gripping her tightly. "I've always needed you. Always."

They moved frantically, anger fueling every thrust, pain mixing with pleasure. Their connection was fierce, desperate, and punishing.

He continued to pound her like a madman. The sounds of sloshing and meat smacking was intensified when she had her first orgasm. This wasn't like other times. It was fast, rough, like they were chasing something neither of them could name.

The bed creaked, as her ass slapped against his thighs, and all that tension between them, the jealousy, the resentment, the years of not saying what they really wanted, burned off with every furious thrust.

"Ohh, fuck. I'm about to cum again. Don't you stop. Don't you dare stop." Terry called back as she bit into the pillow.

She let out loud moan with the second orgasm. Donald leaned forward, still thrusting. He buried his face in her back, biting down just enough to make her gasp.

"You think Peter fucked you good?" he muttered, voice rough and low. "He doesn't know your body like I do."

Donald sat up, slowed his strokes, spit on his thumb and shoved it in her ass. Terry's nails raked down the pillow.

"Yes! Ohh yes! Rotate it," she moaned.

He rotated his thumb in her ass and continued to drive into her deeper, faster. She leaned up and Donald wrapped his free hand tight around her throat.

"You like that? Like when I fucking choke you?"

Terry didn't respond; she just moaned. Then she put her hand between her legs to play with her clit. A third orgasm was on the horizon.

Her moans turned into curses. His grunts turned into growls.

As Terry reached her third climax, she dug her nails into Donald's arm. He felt her water his shaft, and he looked down. The sight of her white cream on his dick, as it went in and out, made it impossible for him not to climax.

"Uhh! Damn," was all Donald could get out before he filled her cavern with his own white cream.

And when they finally came, seconds apart, it felt like they'd pounded the argument right out of each other.

But only for now.

In the next room, Kristal sat frozen on her bed, tears silently streaming down her cheeks as muffled sounds of Donald and Terry's aggressive intimacy filled her ears. Her heart shattered further with every groan, every cry, each noise a painful reminder of her mistake.

"This is bullshit," she whispered bitterly, wiping angrily at her tears. She had somehow allowed herself to become collateral damage.

A soft knock interrupted her thoughts. Julian's cautious voice came through the door. "Kristal? Can I come in?"

She quickly wiped her face. "Yeah."

Julian stepped inside, shutting the door behind him. His expression was gentle, sympathetic.

"You okay?"

"Seriously, Julian? I'm a fucking disaster." She laughed humorlessly.

He sat beside her, gently placing a comforting hand on her shoulder.

"Want to talk about it?"

"What's to talk about? I fucked up," she replied sharply, fresh tears forming. "I let myself catch feelings for Donald, knowing damn well he's married. Married to my best friend of all people. I'm such an idiot."

"You're human," Julian corrected softly. "We all make mistakes and sometimes do dumb shit. There are whole YouTube channels to show it."

"Yeah, well mine's being broadcast loud and fucking clear," she said bitterly. "Now I'm trapped here, forced to listen to their fucked-up attempt to fix things."

Julian sighed deeply. "They're not fixing anything. They're just hurting each other more."

"It doesn't matter," Kristal muttered. "They're married. They'll chose each other. I'm just garbage."

Julian squeezed her shoulder gently. "You deserve better. You deserve someone who chooses you first."

She glanced at him sharply.

"Then why the fuck do I always pick men who never do?"

Julian sighed softly. "Maybe because it's easier to chase someone unavailable than face the risk of being truly loved."

Kristal exhaled, absorbing his words.

"I don't know how to stop."

"You start by believing you deserve more," Julian said gently. "Because you do."

She leaned into him, allowing herself comfort, even as her heart continued to ache from the noises next door.

"Hey, let's go have some drinks in my room until...well, you know," Julian said with a nod towards the wall connected to Donald and Terry's room.

"Yeah, that's a great idea. I can't listen to this shit anymore."

They quickly got up and left, not closing the door.

Outside by the pool, Peter nursed a whiskey, eyes fixed blankly on the water, the distant sounds from upstairs a bitter reminder of his actions. Nia stepped outside, closing the sliding glass door firmly behind her.

"You satisfied, Peter? Happy with what you did?"

Peter glared defensively.

"Don't put this all on me, Nia."

"Who the fuck else should I blame?" she shot back angrily. "You blew up everyone's lives because your ego got bruised. That is petty as hell, even for you."

"They were already fucked up. I didn't cause that. I just pulled back the curtain so everyone could see the same things."

"No, but you sure as hell made it worse," Nia snapped. "You're no fucking hero. You're just bitter. Why? Because no one cares about your huge dick, or the new one rep max on your bench."

"Maybe I am bitter, Nia," he admitted harshly. "But at least I'm honest. They've been lying for months."

"How honest were you?" she challenged. "Did you tell Terry you're in love with her before this, or did you just blow up her marriage for fun?"

Peter tensed, voice tight.

"I didn't mean...I'm not. No, I'm not--"

"Exactly," Nia interrupted. "You didn't think at all. You were jealous and reckless. Now everyone's hurt, including you. You hear them up there? They are going crazy on each other, hiding their feelings with sex. That won't fix anything."

Peter lowered his head.

"Fuck, Nia. What am I supposed to do now?"

"Stop running from your faults," she said. "Own up, apologize, do something productive."

He nodded slowly.

"I fucked everything up this trip."

"Yeah, you did," Nia agreed bluntly. "But maybe you can still do something right."

"Like what?"

Nia softened slightly.

"Start by apologizing. Then, maybe be honest with Terry about your motivations. She might not feel like being around you for a while, but at least everything is out."

He nodded quietly, knowing she was right. The damage was done, but perhaps he could still find a way forward.

Morning arrived too soon, sunlight invading Terry and Donald's room. She lay still, staring blankly at the ceiling, rubbing her still swollen pussy. Beside her, Donald slept uneasily. She quietly slipped from bed and stepped onto the balcony. The cool air soothed her reheated emotions and her pelvis.

Donald joined her moments later, cautious.

"Can we talk?"

"There's nothing left to say," she replied with quiet resignation.

"I never meant to hurt you," he said softly.

"Well, you did anyway," she whispered fiercely, eyes glistening. "Maybe it was easier to pretend our problems weren't there. We just left a small opening and resentment, despair, and complacency slipped in. Rotted the whole thing from the inside."

"I want to fix this," he pleaded gently. He reached for her hand, but she didn't flinch, didn't pull away either.

"Maybe it's too late, Donald. Last night felt great for a while, but maybe it's too late to save anything."

"Don't say that."

"I have to," she whispered. "We can't live in denial anymore. If a woman other than me was able to get to your heart, that screams it might be over."

"But nothing happened. I mean, we get along and have a good time together."

"Donald, I don't know how I can say this to make more sense. If you would've had sex with Kristal, that would be a great betrayal too. But her getting to you emotionally hurts more. I can't explain it, it just does."

Donald quietly shook his head, and Terry walked away.

As afternoon waned, the group gathered around the kitchen table with unspoken pain.

Terry finally spoke, voice weary.

"We all need to face reality. We can't stay like this. We need space. Time apart."

Peter exhaled softly. "Space might be best."

"Agreed," everyone said in unison. But Donald gave Peter a death glare as he said it.

Kristal nodded slowly, regret and understanding clear. She looked down at her juice, lips twisting into a tight mope. She never really had Donald, but somehow, it still felt like losing him.

Julian and Nia exchanged solemn glances.

"It's settled then," Terry said softly. "We leave now and talk later. We need clarity."

A resigned silence settled over them, marking an end to something they had cherished deeply. The future remained uncertain, the pain fresh, but perhaps, in distance, healing would begin.

EPISODE: 14: The Cooldown

Their drive back from the Outer Banks had been quiet. No music. Just the sound of tires on the highway and the occasional sigh from the passenger seat. Donald kept his eyes on the road, staying under the speed limit, like speeding might unravel the last threads holding them together.

They didn't speak much in the days that followed either.

Now, a week later, even that silence had become a strange kind of luxury.

Terry stood in the hallway of their home just before dawn, barefoot on the cold floor, cradling a small overnight bag against her hip. She could hear the hum of the refrigerator in the kitchen, the steady tick of the wall clock above the couch. They were normal sounds, but this morning, they felt exaggerated, like the house itself was waiting for something.

From the cracked bedroom door came the faint rustle of Donald shifting in his sleep. The sound hit her in the chest. Not because it was unusual, but because it was so heartbreakingly normal.

She'd packed the bag slowly, carefully. Only what she needed for a couple nights: toiletries, her favorite soft leggings, the book she kept rereading but never finished. A plain hoodie and her journal zipped into the front pocket. She wanted to be invisible.

She stepped into the living room and glanced toward the couch, half-expecting to see him there, awake, waiting for her to speak first. But it was empty.

Her hand hovered over the doorknob like it was red hot. She looked up and stared at the picture of a man who had once felt like home.

Now he looked like a question she didn't want to answer.

Terry waited until she was outside to breathe fully. The air was damp and cool, the kind of chill that clung to your skin even through a hoodie. She pulled the hood up anyway, not to block the wind, but to create a bubble around her that nothing could enter. The Uber was already parked at the curb, its headlights off.

She slid into the back seat, offered a quiet, "good morning," and leaned back as they drove away.

She gave the name, Terry Brewer, at the front desk of the modest boutique hotel downtown. Her maiden name. She hadn't said it out loud in years. It felt foreign on her tongue, like borrowing someone else's past.

Room 212 was her temporary haven. No grand views, no frills, and no questions from the desk clerk. A room that asked for nothing and gave nothing in return.

She dropped her bag on the stiff bedspread and stood by the window. The city was slowly coming alive outside, bathed in the softest gradient of pale pinks and lavender blue. Morning crept over the horizon like it was afraid to wake the world.

Her phone sat face-up on the table. She reached for it, opened the message app, then stopped. She wasn't ready for conversation.

Instead, she opened the Notes app and typed a single line:

"If this is what peace feels like, why does it hurt more than the fight?"

She stared at the words before locking the screen.

The hotel room smelled like bleach and air conditioning. She pressed her forehead to the cool window and let out a long, tired sigh.

It took her another hour to build the courage to type out the message that had been forming in her head since the Outer Banks.

Terry:

"I need some space. Please don't ask where."

She hit send before she could change her mind.

Back home, Donald's phone buzzed against the nightstand. He sat up slowly, blinking at the brightness of the screen. The bed felt colder and bigger without her.

Terry:

"I need some space. Please don't ask where."

He stared at the words like they were written in a foreign language. His fingers hovered over the keyboard, thumbs twitching as he typed and erased more than once.

Finally, he sent one sentence.

Donald:

"I'll give you that. But I'm not giving up."

Then he dropped the phone face-down and leaned back against the headboard, letting the ceiling fan spin above him as morning broke outside.

Terry sat cross-legged in the scratchy, low-back hotel chair, a lukewarm coffee cupped between both hands like it held the weight of her choices. The taste was bitter and burnt, but she sipped it anyway, letting the warmth ground her in something physical. The kind of small, uncomfortable thing that reminded her she was still here, still breathing, even if she wanted to feel like a ghost.

The city outside the window stirred. A jogger passed by, not a care in the world. A barista propped open the coffee shop door next to the hotel, releasing the faint scent of roasted beans that never quite reached her floor. A delivery truck parked awkwardly on the curb, flashers blinking like a heartbeat.

It all moved on without her. The world didn't know, didn't show, and didn't care that she felt broken.

She'd always imagined that if she ever had to leave her marriage, it would be dramatic. Tears, screaming, maybe even slamming doors and having the cops called because they had disturbed the world.

But in the end, it had been quiet. Surgical. She didn't even leave a note.

About an hour later, her phone buzzed. She picked it up, just a work email. Nothing from Donald. Not that she expected anything. She asked for space, and he was giving it. But his silence still felt like a slap.

She opened her Note again and wrote:

"Why do I feel lighter and lonelier?"

Her fingers hovered before she added:

"Because I finally stepped away. But not forward."

A third line came unbidden:

"Distance doesn't always equal clarity. Sometimes it just echoes."

Terry closed her screen and stood too fast, her blood rushing to her head. She caught herself on the chair and let out a curse under her breath. "Damn."

There was no epiphany coming. No bolt of clarity striking her from the 212th window of a 3-star hotel. It was just time, space, and herself.

Meanwhile, across the city, Donald moved like he was sleepwalking.

He brushed his teeth without looking in the mirror. His reflection felt like a stranger. Some alternate version he didn't want to make eye contact with. He made his protein shake, drank half, and tossed the rest.

***

The gym was crowded, but he kept to himself: Bench press, squats, deadlifts, and lunges. Donald attacked bench and leg day on a Monday like he was punishing himself. His body ached in all the right ways by the end of the session, but none of it touched the hollowness in his chest.

He didn't text Terry. He wanted to. But every draft felt either too needy or dismissive. "Thinking of you," sounded cliché. "I miss you," felt like a trap. "I'm sorry," was too little, too late. So, he said nothing.

He went home, showered, and sat on the edge of the bed staring at the spot she used to sleep in. His imagination was refusing to let go.

Later, after dark, he decided to walk, no destination.

A breeze kicked up along the sidewalk, rustling loose leaves and whipping the collar of his shirt against his neck. His mind wandered to the last night in Outer Banks. To Terry's silence. To the way Kristal had looked at him across the fire pit. Sympathy mixed with something else he couldn't name.

On impulse, he turned down a street near his job. A small café, The Cozy Cup, sat tucked between a yoga studio and a stationery shop. He'd seen it dozens of times and never stopped.

Tonight, he did.

The electric bell over the café door gave a soft song as Donald stepped inside, brushing his hand over the back of his neck. The scent hit him like a memory: warm Chai, roasted espresso, steamed milk, a hint of cardamom and brown sugar. Comfort. Safety.

The café was cozy, not staged or aesthetic like the newer places. The walls were lined with reclaimed wood shelves stuffed with mismatched mugs and potted succulents. A couple sat tucked into a corner booth over a shared slice of cake. Someone was sketching at a high table, earbuds in, focused.

Donald shuffled toward the counter.

"Chai tea. Hot. No sugar," he said. His voice sounded distant, like it didn't belong to him.

"Name?"

He almost said hers.

"Ter...Donald," he corrected.

The barista nodded and turned away.

He exhaled. And that's when he saw her.

Kristal.

She was by the back window, alone. One foot tucked under her, book in hand, latte slowly steaming beside her. Her oversized sweater fell off one shoulder in that effortless way some women seemed born with. A gold hoop earring caught the light when she shifted slightly. She wasn't trying to be noticed. She just was.

Her eyes lifted, casual and unbothered, until they locked onto his.

Then they weren't casual at all.

They froze. Something old and something unspoken pulsed between them. Donald's pulse jumped in his neck.

She gave him a small nod, lips pressing into the ghost of a smile. He returned it, the corner of his mouth lifting involuntarily.

The barista broke the trance.

"Order for Donald."

"Thanks," Donald replied as he grabbed it, fingers brushing the cardboard sleeve like it could distract him from what was happening in his chest.

Kristal gestured to the seat across from her with a tilt of her head. It was unassuming, not a command, nor plea. Just an opening.

He took it.

"Small world," he said sliding onto the seat.

Kristal closed the book and leaned her chin into her palm. "More like big city with only a handful of decent cafés."

"You know, I've passed this place a dozen times and never came in." Donald grinned.

She raised an eyebrow. "So, you finally took a chance tonight?"

He sipped his tea. "Apparently. Yeah, I'm doing that more often lately."

They lapsed into silence for a moment. Not awkward. Just allowing the space to breathe.

"I heard about what happened after the trip," she said quietly.

Donald tilted his head.

"Terry talk to you?"

She shook her head. "Not really. Just vibes. And Peter. He's been... rant-adjacent lately."

"I figured." Donald sighed.

Kristal studied his face for a moment. Her voice was soft.

"You always get this look when you're hurting. Your mouth gets tight, but your eyes don't lie."

He looked down at his tea.

"You notice that, huh?"

She shrugged.

"I've always noticed you. Just didn't say it out loud."

He looked back at her, something sharp and easy all at once playing behind his eyes.

"You told me once you liked me more when I was sad."

"Because the sad you is real. No jokes. No 'I'm fine.' Just... honest."

"That's messed up," he muttered with a smile.

She laughed lightly. "It is. But so is everything right now."

Donald leaned back in the chair, letting the tea warm his chest.

"You know what I miss? Quiet mornings. Knowing who I was waking up to. Even the smell of her perfume on the pillow."

Kristal's face softened.

"Then why does it feel like you're not trying to get that back?"

He paused.

"I think part of me knows...it's already gone. We're both just staring at the ashes hoping they catch flame again."

Kristal reached out and touched his wrist. It was subtle but electric. He didn't move away.

They sat there, fingers barely connected, the rest of the world blurring into static.

"You still pretend to read when you don't want to be approached?" Donald asked, eyeing the book beside her.

Kristal smirked. "Better than pretending to be emotionally available."

"Touché," he smirked.

She laughed. The kind of laugh that made it clear she wasn't bluffing.

Her hand lingered. Her thumb brushed the inside of his wrist gently, like a memory she didn't want to lose.

When she finally pulled away, the space between them felt colder.

"It's weird," she whispered. "You know, how the world keeps spinning even when yours flips upside down."

Donald nodded slowly, eyeing the remnants of his hot tea.

Eventually, they both stood. She adjusted her sweater. He grabbed his keys.

They didn't plan to walk out together, and they didn't.

Donald stepped into the night air, blinking under the streetlamp's glow. The breeze tugged at the hem of his shirt as the warmth of Kristal's touch tugged on his mind.

He started walking. It wasn't fast and had no direction. He just wanted to go far enough.

His phone buzzed in his pocket. He pulled it out and glared at the screen.

Terry:

"You still thinking about us?"

He reread it like it was written in another language.

His fingers hovered.

He typed, deleted. Typed again.

Finally, he sent:

"Every day."

Then he slid the phone into his pocket, exhaled, and kept walking.

The tea had gone cold in his chest. But his pulse was starting to burn again.

EPISODE: 15: Friction and Fire

The hotel room was quiet, almost too quiet.

Terry rested on her side in the stiff, over-bleached sheets of the suite, staring at the black digital clock, 2 a.m. Her eyes burned, but sleep wouldn't come. Not here. Not now.

She turned over again, the pillow was cool against her cheek. Still, no peace. Her body was tired, but her mind spun like it had cocaine for blood.

Memories weren't kind to her. They didn't ask permission. They kicked down the door and barged in.

Maine: The fireplace had been crackling as Kristal twirled in that tight dress, laughing. The smell of cinnamon and wood smoke billowed. Peter lifted her effortlessly into the hot tub while Donald poured drinks. Laughter and nervousness reverberated like innocence. A flicker—Kristal bent forward in the hot tub, the swell of her cleavage in that neon red bikini top catching Donald's eye. Terry hadn't thought anything of it then. But now...

Now, she remembered how Donald's eyes lingered a second too long.

"Was it always there? Did I miss that invisible line between them?" Terry thought.

She sat up, pressing her fingers to her temples. She wasn't normally a jealous woman, but this situation made her normal disappear.

Something was breaking. And the worst part? She couldn't even say when the first crack appeared.

Her phone buzzed against the nightstand, startling her.

Kristal:

"Please. I just want to talk. I don't want it to end this way."

Terry stared at the screen, her lips parting like she might say something out loud to a ghost.

Another buzz.

Kristal:

"Please."

Terry didn't answer. Not yet.

She got up and paced, the hotel carpet rough under her bare feet. Her reflection in the window stared back at her. A woman too tired to be strong but too angry to crumble.

The phone buzzed again.

Kristal:

"Please. Just talking. I know it's hard, but we've been friends too long for it to end like this."

Terry finally typed, fingers flying before she could second-guess the words.

Terry:

"Then you should've thought about that before trying to steal my fucking husband."

The reply came fast.

Kristal:

"It's not like that. Just meet me."

Terry tossed the phone onto the bed, arms crossed. She stared at it like it might explode.

Minutes passed. Then an hour. Then two.

She checked her phone again. Still nothing more from Kristal.

Her thumb hovered over the reply field. Then she typed:

Terry:

"One hour. And pick a public place."

No emoji. No kindness.

Just rules.

She dropped the phone back onto the bed and reached for her coat. If Kristal wanted to talk, she'd get her chance.

But not in private. And not without consequences.

The wind off the river carried a damp chill, the kind that bit through denim and pride alike.

Terry stood near the park's stone overlook, arms folded across her chest, posture sharp with tension. Behind her, the water shimmered beneath a hazy half-moon. The air smelled like damp bark and last night's rain, moody, unsettled. Late joggers passed at a distance, giving them space. It was quiet, but not private. Perfect for a confrontation.

Kristal arrived six minutes late.

She walked with uncertain steps, sneakers crunching on the gravel path. Her oversized hoodie looked like a shield she wanted to hide behind. No makeup, hair in a low bun, eyes shadowed with exhaustion. She looked like someone who'd been crying into her pillow but hadn't allowed herself the comfort of sleep.

Terry didn't move.

Kristal stopped a few feet away and exhaled like she'd just ran a mile.

"Hey."

Terry's eyes narrowed.

"You gonna fuck him next, or just keep sipping your lattes in slow motion while you imagine it? I mean hell I was already dumb enough to let it happen right in front of me I guess."

Kristal flinched.

"Terry..."

"You don't get to 'Terry' me," she snapped. "You get to explain. What we did before was...was impulsive and just some onetime thing. This is just unbelievable."

"I'm not trying to take Donald from you."

Terry cocked her head.

"Then tell me you didn't lean in. Tell me you didn't enjoy the way he looked at you."

Kristal opened her mouth, then shut it. Her silence said everything.

"That's what I thought bitch," Terry said, stepping forward, voice low and biting. "You liked it. The attention. The possibility. You couldn't just leave what happened in the past."

Kristal's lips trembled.

"It wasn't supposed to mean anything. I don't even think about him in that way. We just... we talked."

"Talked? Is that what we're calling flirting now?" Terry snorted.

"It wasn't like that, Terry. I was lonely. I still am. I wasn't thinking about us having sex or being together, I just wanted someone to hear me."

"And Donald was convenient? Familiar? All the things that I, your best friend are?"

Kristal's voice grew firmer.

"He was kind. You are my best friend, but sometimes you can be a little...intimidating. I know you don't mean too, but it just feels like I'm your little sister sometimes. I don't always feel confident bringing you my problems."

Terry blinked. Kristal's words hit harder than she expected.

"I didn't go looking for him," Kristal said. "He was just... there. Listening. Not judging. It wasn't about stealing anything. I just made a new friend, and he happened to be your husband."

"But you did steal," Terry said. "Whether you meant to or not, you stole comfort that didn't belong to you. That shouldn't belong to you."

Kristal's hands curled into fists at her sides.

"You think I feel good about this? Like I woke up and decided to fuck over the only people who ever made me feel like family?"

"You tell me," Terry said, the anger finally spilling through her calm facade. "You've always been that girl, Kristal. The one who smiles a little too long. Hugs a little too close. Looks at people like they're a secret she wants to keep."

"I never tried to seduce him."

"No, you just let him seduce you." Terry's voice cracked like dry wood.

Kristal stared at her, blinking back tears.

"You're not being fair."

"Fair? Neither are you."

A gust of wind fluttered the hem of Kristal's hoodie. The silence swelled, swollen with all the things they hadn't said for years.

Terry took another step forward, eyes gleaming.

"Are you fucking him? Not some random wild shit. I mean, are you two..." Terry stopped and just stared at Kristal with incensed eyes.

"No. We aren't fucking, Terry."

"Did you think I wouldn't find out?"

Kristal sighed.

"There's nothing to find out!" She blurted out getting louder. "We enjoy each other's comfort by talking, that's it. I didn't expect it to feel this... heavy."

"Did you love him back then too?" Terry's voice cracked. "Or did you just wait for the first sign of cracks so you could slip in like a parasite?"

Kristal gasped like a slap had already landed. "I never said I love him. And that's not fair. A parasite, really Terry?"

"You never said you loved him, but you can't deny it either, can you? Your little private conversations back then should have clued me in." Terry said.

Kristal's voice trembled.

"You don't know what it was like with Peter. What it's like to sleep beside someone who forgets you're alive. Not everything is about sex. Donald was kind to me. That's all it was at first."

"At first," Terry repeated, venom laced into the words. "And now?"

Kristal opened her mouth then closed it. There was nothing left to say that wouldn't deepen the wound.

Terry turned and started to walk away.

"Stay the fuck away from him," she muttered, not looking back. Her voice was low, but it struck like a whip.

Kristal didn't follow. She just stood there, shivering under the weight of the moment, watching Terry disappear into the blur of the city.

For the first time in years, Kristal didn't feel like the bubbly, beautiful, life of the party. She just felt empty.

Kristal walked toward her car, then sat down on the park bench long after Terry had vanished. She stared blankly at the water, willing her pulse to slow down. But Terry's words still ricocheted in her chest like tiny explosions.

"You liked when he looked at you."

"You just waited for cracks so you could slip in like a parasite."

Each line hit harder than the last.

She wiped at her face, realizing she'd been crying. Again. She hated crying in public. Hated this sudden unraveling of the woman she'd spent years pretending to be, unbothered, unbreakable, desired but detached.

Now, the mask had fallen, and in its place was just Kristal. Raw. Seen. Complicated.

Her phone buzzed in her hoodie pocket. She didn't even want to look, but the screen flashed:

Nia:

"Y'all good? Park meetup felt like a bad episode of Insecure. Just saying."

Kristal let out a weak, humorless laugh. Leave it to Nia to sniff out drama like a bloodhound. She had been through her own issues, and humor was Nia's best defense from feeling.

She didn't respond.

Instead, she pulled her knees up on the bench and hugged them to her chest like she used to do in college when the world felt too loud.

Meanwhile, across town, Terry stepped back into her hotel room and dropped her keys onto the dresser like they'd burned her. The moment the door clicked shut, the tears came fast and without permission.

She didn't bother turning on the lights. She sat on the edge of the bed, hands trembling, her own words echoing in her head now.

"Tell me you didn't enjoy the way he looked at you."

"Did you love him back then too?"

She hated that she'd asked. Hated that a part of her still needed to know because deep down, Terry wasn't just angry about Kristal. She was furious at herself for seeing it coming and doing nothing. For thinking Kristal was too polished, too poised, too perfect to ever crave something as average as Donald.

And yet. It had happened.

Terry stared at the ceiling, the emotional weight crushing her like a hydraulic press.

There were no more tears. Just the heavy, hollow ache of betrayal shared equally between the man she married and the friend she'd once sworn would stand beside her at every major milestone.

She didn't know which betrayal hurt more. But she knew neither wound would heal clean.

Her phone buzzed on the nightstand. Another text from Nia.

Nia:

"Ok but deadass, did y'all throw hands ���� or just ruin each other emotionally like grown women?"

Terry snorted. She wasn't sure if it was from exhaustion or genuine amusement.

She picked up the phone and replied.

Terry:

"No fists. Just weapons-grade honesty."

Nia:

"😳😳😳That's worse tbh. Y'all okay?"

Terry hesitated:

Terry:

"No. But I think I needed to say it."

Nia:

"Cool. Now please don't die of stress before Friendsgiving. I already bought a dress that shows side boob."

Terry let out a short, surprised laugh. It was barely a sound, but it was something.

Terry:

"No promises."

Nia:

"Fair. But if I gotta choose between y'all's drama and green bean casserole, I'm siding with carbs."

Terry dropped the phone onto her chest, staring at the ceiling again.

For the first time all day, the ache in her chest eased, slightly. Not enough to forget, but enough to breathe.

EPISODE: 16: Lines Crossed

Terry didn't go back to the house for a few days.

She stayed in her modest hotel room on the edge of the city. A mid-range chain with burnt-orange accent walls, a microwave no one trusted, and curtains that never quite shut all the way. The bedspread smelled faintly of bleach and someone else's decisions. It wasn't comfortable, but it was anonymous. It didn't ask her to explain anything, and she was grateful for that.

She didn't communicate with Donald, but she didn't block him either. She just went silent, like a signal lost in a storm.

The night after the park, she lay in bed fully dressed, the hotel air conditioner humming inconsistently like it had opinions. Her phone buzzed once. Then again. Then three more times, all from Donald. She didn't check. She let the messages rot in the notification bar.

When morning came, it wasn't a sunrise it was an unwelcome brightness. She dragged herself to the little armchair by the window and stared out at the parking lot. The sky was a chalky blue, already heating up with city steam. People went in and out of the lobby, hauling suitcases, wearing earbuds, living normal lives. A normal she no longer recognized.

A notebook was open in her lap, the pen hovering but refusing to move. She wrote one sentence.

"Why do I feel lighter and lonelier?"

Then she shut the journal and left it face down on the side table.

She didn't eat much throughout the day, a banana here, vending machine granola bar there. Most nights she just stared at the ceiling, the popcorn texture becoming a map she kept tracing, hoping it would show her where she went wrong.

When she finally decided to go home, it was strategic. She knew Donald would be at work. She'd memorized his schedule in a way that still irritated her, even now.

She parked two blocks away; her keys clutched tightly in her hand as she walked toward the building. Every step felt like trespassing.

Inside, everything looked the same but wrong. Her throw blanket was still draped across the couch, but someone had folded it differently. The bathroom smelled like his cologne. The hand towel was folded with more care than she ever gave it. He was trying. That part made it worse.

She went into the bedroom, opened the closet, and stood there.

Half her things were already gone. Not because she'd taken them but because she'd stopped leaving parts of herself there months ago. The drawers that used to overflow with her scarves, her scented oils, her journals; they now held only silence.

She grabbed her favorite hoodie first, the one she wore the day Donald proposed. Then the navy heels she bought after her first nursing promotion. She placed them gently in her duffel, like they deserved better than this.

Piece by piece, she unraveled herself from the space.

On the dresser, she placed a folded note:

"I'm not sure I want to fix us anymore. Not if I'm the only one doing the work."

No "love," no "goodbye." Just finality.

She lingered at the door before leaving, her eyes glancing toward the small photo on the entryway table. The Polaroid from Maine. All four of them, side by side. Laughing. Sun-kissed. Untouched by reality.

She walked over to it, lifted it slowly, ran her finger along the glass. Her face in the photo looked younger. Or maybe just more certain.

She flipped the picture down with a soft clack and left without locking the door behind her.

She didn't know if she'd ever be back.

***

Kristal didn't expect to see him.

She'd gone to the downtown art walk for distraction, not disaster. The city had cracked open into twilight, bathed in warm lavender light that streaked across the sky like faded brushstrokes. Streetlights flickered on slowly, one by one, as if trying to catch up to the buzz of people milling about the cobblestone square.

Pop-up art booths stretched along the sidewalks, each one glowing from strings of Edison bulbs. The air smelled of roasted almonds, cheap wine, and new acrylic paint. Musicians set up on the corners; one strumming a melancholy acoustic riff that threaded the scene together with background music from a breakup montage.

Kristal wore something simple, a white tank, vintage jeans, a denim jacket slung around her waist. Her curls were caught up in a lazy knot, a few spirals escaping near her ear. Still, she had that quiet, broken-glass kind of glow, sharp, beautiful, and reflecting too much.

She sipped a plastic cup of chardonnay and squinted at a display of abstract canvases, bold orange slashes over brooding blue storms. It felt chaotic and strangely familiar to her own thoughts painted across someone else's skin.

She was about to move on when she saw, Donald.

He stood several booths away, brows furrowed, hands tucked into his hoodie pockets. He wasn't watching her, yet. But he looked like a man trying hard to focus on something that didn't matter, probably failing at it. His hair had grown out slightly, curls tighter, and there was a heaviness in the slope of his shoulders.

He lifted his head to walk to the next booth and their eyes met across the space.

And just like that, something tightened.

They both looked away, then back again.

Kristal didn't move. She just watched him edge closer. Not deliberate. But not accidental either.

"You didn't strike me as the art walk type," she said as he reached the booth.

Donald glanced at the painting beside her.

"Didn't think I was either. But this one... it won't shut up."

Kristal cocked her head toward the canvas.

"Yeah, it's loud. But kind of haunting too."

"Like it's arguing with itself." He nodded.

They stood side by side, not touching. The crowd swirled around them laughing couples, clinking glasses, children weaving through adult legs. But here, in this sliver of stillness, they may as well have been alone.

"You okay?" she asked, her voice soft but steady.

Donald exhaled through his nose.

"I'm somewhere between tired and too awake."

Kristal glanced down at her wine.

"Same."

He looked at her then. Not just at her outfit or her face, but all of her—eyes, posture, breath. It was the kind of look that said he wasn't over anything.

She lowered her eyes.

"You look like you're carrying too much."

"Feels that way." He shrugged, lips tight.

The breeze picked up, tugging at the edges of her jacket and bringing the scent of rain-soaked asphalt and late-night coffee. She closed her eyes for a second. Just one. But when she opened them, he was still there.

"I saw Terry," she said.

He tensed slightly but said nothing.

"She said some things."

"Hmm. Did she hit you?"

Kristal blinked, surprised.

"No."

"Then it wasn't that bad."

Kristal almost laughed. "She said you look at me differently. That it's always been there, even if I didn't want to see it."

Donald didn't answer.

"Is she wrong," Kristal whispered.

Silence.

Kristal leaned against the table behind her, fingers running along the edge of a ceramic sculpture shaped like tangled limbs.

"You ever feel like you're already paying for sins you haven't committed yet?"

"Every damn day." Donald's response was low, guttural.

They stood in that shared ache for a moment longer.

"You scare me," she said finally.

"Scare you. Why?"

"Because you make me want things I thought I buried."

Donald stepped closer, not enough to alarm, but enough to change the air. Her pulse jumped.

"You're not the only one."

She touched his wrist. Just barely. Her fingers rested there for a moment like they were remembering something together. Then she pulled away first, letting the contact dissolve into the space between them.

Kristal's look drifted to the canvas beside them, the one they'd both been staring at without really seeing. The tangled shapes almost looked like bodies locked together, straining toward something unseen.

Donald followed her line of sight.

"You like it?" he asked.

"It's... intense." Her voice was quiet, almost cautious. "Like it knows what's going on in the world."

He huffed out a small laugh. "Guess that means it's honest."

"Or dangerous." Kristal added.

The painting they'd both stared at for far too long followed them home. Donald purchased it quietly, speaking to the vendor while Kristal stood to the side, arms folded across her chest like a shield. The artist wrapped the large canvas in a plastic shell, taping the edges, muttering something about "trauma and rebirth" and how the piece was called Ashes Don't Apologize.

Donald asked Kristal if she'd help him get it to the house. She hesitated, then nodded, yes.

Donald took the longer route home, windows cracked, letting in the buzz of city life and a summer night's restlessness. Kristal followed in her car, her headlights a silent echo trailing him through the streets.

At the house, he turned the alarm off and propped the door open. The air inside was still and familiar, the faint scent of Terry's lavender diffuser still clinging to the hall, though the oil had run dry days ago.

Kristal walked in slowly, holding one side of the painting.

They leaned the uncovered painting against the living room wall. Donald stepped back to look at it again. The sharp colors looked different in the warm light of the house. The reds felt angrier. The blue streaks, colder.

"You want wine?" he asked.

Kristal gave him a small nod and followed him to the kitchen.

They stood in the kitchen as he poured two glasses. The wine was deep, dark, something he had left over from the holidays. Kristal took a sip and leaned against the counter, eyes trailing the edge of the marble.

"This house feels like her," she said softly.

Donald didn't argue.

They migrated back into the living room. The painting loomed behind them like a witness. Kristal sat on the couch first. Donald joined her, careful to leave space.

A few more sips in, the silence grew heavier. It wasn't awkward. It was anticipation, thick enough to chew.

Kristal turned toward him.

"Do you ever stop feeling guilty?"

Donald's jaw flexed.

"Only when I'm asleep. And lately, I don't sleep much."

She set her glass down. "I hated that I felt seen by you. Because it meant something. And it shouldn't."

He took a deep breath. "You were always seen. You just forgot how to let it happen."

Their faces were inches apart.

Kristal whispered, "say something that'll make me walk away."

"I can't."

She closed the gap.

The kiss was slow—not desperate or fevered but soaked in exhaustion and need. Like they were sipping from something forbidden but essential. His hand brushed her jaw. Hers curled around his shirt, pulling him close, but not all the way.

They kissed for what felt like hours but couldn't have been more than minutes.

When they finally parted, Kristal didn't speak. She rested her forehead against his.

"Well, that won't help matters at all." Donald whispered.

"No," she breathed. "But I'm not sorry."

"If we do this," he said slowly, "there's no walking it back."

Kristal leaned back just enough to see his face.

"I know."

Donald's thumb brushed her cheek, lingering just long enough to make her breath catch.

"Then you should go," he said softly. "Before we forget why we can't."

She gave a small nod, but her eyes stayed locked on his like she might stay anyway. Her fingers flexed once at her side, like they were fighting the urge to reach for him.

" I think I'm going to go," she said as she stood up stepping back slightly.

Her bag was already in hand; strap looped over her shoulder like she might need to run. At the door, she looked back not tender or apologetic, but with a spark that promised trouble. Then she was gone, heels clicking against the pavement until her car swallowed her whole.

After watching Kristal walk away, back inside, Donald sank into the couch.

The painting stared back at him from across the room. The house was quiet and still again, like so many nights the past couple of weeks.

Then his phone buzzed.

Terry:

"You still want us?"

He didn't answer at first. His thumb hovered over the keyboard.

He typed: "Of course."

Deleted it.

Typed: "I never stopped."

Deleted again.

His eyes drifted to the coffee table. Kristal's wine glass still sat there. A faint imprint of lipstick circled the rim like a kiss that hadn't finished fading.

He sighed.

Then he typed something simple. But didn't send it.

Kristal's lipstick was still on the wine glass. The actual kiss was still on his lips. And Terry's words were still in his hands.

EPISODE: 17: What We Break

Donald stirred before the sun rose.

The room was dim, bathed in pale gray light, like the world itself hadn't decided what kind of day it wanted to be. His body ached not from labor or workouts, but from the weight of choices made in silence and sealed with a kiss.

He rolled onto his back; the sheets tangled like regret around his legs. For a moment, he watched at the ceiling, unmoving, not even blinking. It felt like if he moved too quickly, the whole thing would unravel—his marriage, his memories, the fragile piece of quiet he had managed to clutch through the night.

The phone on the nightstand buzzed. He reached for it like it was something sharp.

It wasn't a new message. Just a reminder. Terry's last words still sat there, unanswered:

"You still want us?"

He hadn't replied.

Not because he didn't have an answer, but because he had too many.

He tapped into the thread. Stared at it again and highlighted the words like they were a wound, reopening. Then swiped the screen dark.

He rose slowly, padding barefoot to the kitchen. The light in there was warmer, softer. It didn't feel as judgmental as the bedroom.

He poured himself a glass of water, took one long sip as he walked to the living room, and set it down beside something he thought he had put away.

The wine glass.

Just one.

Her lipstick was gone now. He wasn't sure if he had washed it himself or if he'd rubbed it off with his thumb last night in a moment of conflicted panic. Either way, the smudge was gone, but the aftertaste wasn't.

He sat at the counter, rubbing his temples with one hand, letting the silence linger. It was a hollow kind of quietness that echoed, even without a sound.

Everything felt a little off.

His routine was the same. The kitchen the same. But there was a hair tie in the hallway, a small one that he didn't know if it belonged to Kristal or Terry. It made him pause. Because now, everything in the house made him think of what wasn't supposed to happen, and what still might.

He got dressed for the gym, gray joggers, a hoodie, and a scuffed black hat Terry always used to steal and wear around the house when she was cleaning or cooking. He hesitated before pulling it on, then stuffed it into a drawer instead.

"No ghosts today. Just sweat."

He needed something to burn other than guilt.

The gym was louder than usual. The clank of iron, the buzz of earbuds, the occasional grunt of ego being tested. It all blended into a kind of background numbness. Just what Donald needed.

He pushed through five sets of bench press and tried to keep his head down. But the weight wasn't enough to shut off the loop in his brain. Kristal's breath against his neck, Terry's message sitting in his pocket like a stone.

"Damn," a voice snapped behind him. "Didn't expect to see Sad Boy Summer on the cables today."

Donald didn't even have to turn around.

"Nia."

She leaned one hip against the cable machine, water bottle tucked under one arm, chewing gum like it owed her rent. Auburn braids pulled into a high bun, sharp eyeliner, and an expression that could cut drywall.

"You look like someone just realized they got caught up in the wrong story," she said, giving him a once-over.

He offered her a dry smile, towel wiping the back of his neck.

"Nah. Just reading the ending before I was ready."

Nia chuckled, short and knowing.

"That's the problem with skipping ahead. You miss the part where the characters make the worst decisions."

Donald shook his head, not denying it.

"You always got a metaphor loaded, huh?"

"Someone's gotta narrate the downfall." She shrugged.

There was a moment of silence between them, filled only by the clanking of machines and muffled rap lyrics from someone's headphones. Nia's gaze softened just a little.

"You good?" she asked, quieter now.

Donald shrugged, then finally said, "I kissed her."

Nia didn't flinch.

"You mean Kristal?"

"Yeah," he nodded.

"Well... shit," she said, exhaling. "Guess that means you already picked your cliff to fall off."

Donald didn't answer.

"You tell Terry?"

He shook his head, no.

She clicked her tongue.

"You really gonna make her find out the hard way?"

"I don't know what I'm doing," he admitted. "It's like... part of me wants to fix it. The other part thinks it's already broken. It's been broken for a while, but we kept putting Band-Aids on it. All I'm doing now is sweeping glass in the dark."

"Then maybe stop walking barefoot," she said, and turned to leave.

Donald watched her walk away, unbothered. She didn't look back, but her words stayed long after she disappeared around the row of treadmills.

***

The hotel room hummed with the kind of quiet that clung to the walls like humidity. Terry sat curled on the corner of the bed, the comforter balled around her knees, phone gripped like a lifeline she didn't want to call.

But she did.

Peter answered on the third ring.

"Hey."

His voice was calm, not surprised. He always hoped she'd call. That was the annoying thing, he had to wait on her to come to him.

"You said something the other day," she began, skipping past pleasantries. "About Kristal smiling. What did you mean?"

"Exactly what the hell I said. She's been glowing lately. And not from yoga."

Terry let out a breath, barely audible.

"You think she's sleeping with Donald?"

"No," he said finally. "Not yet. But they're already closer than they should be."

Terry swallowed, the words tasting bitter. "Did you do all of this because you want me?"

Another pause. This one longer.

"Yes. And no. I mean... yeah, I do. But that's not why I told you."

"Then why?"

Peter's voice came quieter now, not soft, just real.

"Because I've been that guy before. You know, confused, selfish, emotionally absent. I didn't cheat on Kristal. But I might as well have. I stopped showing up. Stopped being with her even though I was right there. Ya know?"

"Ohh yeah. I know."

Peter continued, "I spent so long just fucking women who loved getting destroyed by my dick, my look, the fantasy. And with Kristal... I forgot how to actually be with someone. For real."

"I get it," she murmured. "We all faked happy for too long."

"Yeah. And now look at us, burned bridges and second chances that feel like traps."

"At least you had a bridge. I feel like I was trying to patch one made of duct tape and dreams." Terry gave a bitter laugh.

Peter chuckled.

"That sounds like a lyric. You writing songs now?"

She smiled for the first time in days. It was brief, crooked, but it reached her eyes.

"Thanks, for answering," she said.

"Anytime."

When the call ended, the stillness that returned was gentler. Still heavy, but no longer unbearable.

Terry stared at her phone, then grabbed her keys and headed out the door. She didn't text or call. She just showed up.

The knock was firm, decisive. Like she had already rehearsed this moment a dozen times and now wanted it over with.

Donald opened the door, wearing a wrinkled T-shirt and basketball shorts. He looked like a man who hadn't slept right in days. When he saw her standing there, makeup-free, eyes hollow but locked in, he froze.

Terry stepped inside, brushing past him without a word.

"Yeah, sure, come on in," he muttered, clicking the door shut behind her.

They stood in the living room, surrounded by the mess of real life: a pile of unopened mail, an empty coffee mug on the side table, the scent of detergent still clinging to the air. A damp towel was slung over a chair. A framed photo of them sat on the hallway table, one she didn't remember taking. But what caught her eye was the wine glass still sitting there, half-finished, the faint smear of something around the rim.

Her stomach dropped. She looked at him, her voice low and sharp.

"Have you kissed her?"

Donald's jaw flexed.

"Yes."

Terry took a deep breath, but she didn't look away.

"Was it worth it?" she asked. "Was lusting after my friend worth it?"

His answer came slower this time.

"No. But I can't lie. I needed it."

Terry's face didn't change, but something inside her folded.

Donald continued. "We're married. And yeah, marriages have seasons. But we were in a dry one, and I was the only one watering anything. You stopped talking. Stopped touching me. Stopped even noticing when I came home late. If it wasn't for role play we wouldn't even have had sex."

Her eyes welled, but the tears didn't fall.

"You pulled away long before Kristal came into focus," he added. "I wasn't looking for her. But she saw me when I didn't even know I was still visible."

Terry exhaled sharp and shaky. She looked down at the floor, the hardwood suddenly more interesting than anything in the room.

"You didn't seem to care, Terry. Not until someone else saw me the way you used to."

Terry blinked fast. One tear slipped free before she caught it with her palm.

"And you—" she started, voice cracking, "—you kissed the one person I trusted to be neutral. You kissed the only one I thought wouldn't."

Donald stepped closer but didn't touch her.

"You broke something I was barely holding together," she whispered. "And the worst part? I actually understand why."

She swallowed hard. Her shoulders dropped. All the fight melted into quiet surrender.

She continued. "I gave up on us in my own way. I shut the door and dared you to knock." Terry nodded at her statement, as if that was all she came for; truth, even if it hurt.

Her eyes flicked to the wine glass on the table, the faint imprint catching in the afternoon light. She didn't touch it, didn't speak of it, just looked. Long enough for Donald to notice.

Then she turned and walked away. Donald watched her hand hover over the doorknob, one last pause, then opened it. She didn't glance back as she walked over the threshold. Just the sound of footsteps and a final click that closed more than just the door.

The house was quiet again.

Donald stood for a long time in the same spot she left him, her words still floating in the room, as if they had soaked into the drywall. The calm buzzed like static, like something unresolved that refused to die quietly.

On the kitchen counter sat the unopened container of Terry's favorite green tea. Next to it, the framed photo from their third anniversary, slightly askew. They had looked so happy with matching outfits, genuine smiles, arms tangled like they had a future worth betting on.

He turned it face-down and walked back to the bedroom.

Hours passed before he noticed the key. It sat right in the middle of the dining table, next to a note she hadn't said a word about.

He picked it up. It was folded neatly, no seal. Her handwriting looped across the page like a song that had once meant something.

"I loved you more than I showed you. And I'm sorry for that. I forgive you. I just can't forgive myself for giving Kristal the option of you."

No signature.

No plea.

Just a full stop.

He didn't move for several minutes. Just held the letter in one hand and the key in the other, like both weighed a hundred pounds.

Outside, the wind had picked up. A few leaves brushed against the windowpane, scratching faintly like fingernails on glass.

Eventually, he placed the letter back on the table and walked to the door. Opened it. Closed it again without stepping out just to hear the sound.

The door didn't slam. It whispered shut like it knew something he didn't.

EPISODE: 18: Everything, All at Once

Donald parked three blocks away from the hotel, early dusk light dimming edges of the street. He wasn't sure if it was guilt or instinct that made him do it. The city's soft hum of a Thursday evening surrounded him.

He moved like a man running from a thought he couldn't kill, hat pulled low, sunglasses on despite the fading light.

Kristal had texted the number and a single word: Room 207. Ready.

The carpet in the lobby was patterned in red and gold, faded from years of footsteps. A muted TV hummed from behind the front desk. Donald avoided the clerk's eyes and climbed the stairs two at a time. His heart thumped like he was stealing something.

Kristal stood by the window, soft reflections casting on the glass. The silence stretched long, filled only by the hum of the air conditioning and random sounds from outside that snuck into the room. She hadn't even taken her shoes off yet because she wasn't sure Donald would come.

Then a soft knock. Three short taps.

Kristal opened the door before he could knock again.

She didn't say anything at first. Just looked at him like she'd been holding her breath since the last time she saw him.

"You made it," she said.

"I said I would."

"Well, come in silly. I don't think I bite," Kristal finally showing a smile.

Donald walked in and Kristal closed the door, slowly.

Inside, the room was small but warm. The faint scent of pine cleaner and old air bounced from the walls. There was one queen bed, golden lighting, and an untouched bottle of wine sweating on the desk beside two plastic cups. The curtains were drawn, letting in just a blade of light from outside.

Kristal wore soft joggers and a black fitted tee that clung just slightly to the curve of her waist. She wore no makeup; hair pulled back in a messy bun. She looked like herself stripped of pretense, yet somehow radiant.

"I told myself I just wanted to talk," she said, fingers brushing the edge of the desk. "But then I saw you...and talking just doesn't feel like enough anymore." She trailed off.

"I wasn't sure if I should come either," he said, moving closer. "But then I realized I wasn't sure about anything anymore."

He cupped her cheek gently, and her breath caught. "You nervous?"

She nodded, yes. "Only because I know what we're about to do can't be undone."

She reached for his hand and led him to the bed.

They sat on the edge of the bed, strangers and soulmates in equal measure. Silence that filled the air between them didn't feel heavy, it felt necessary. The wine stayed unopened. Their bodies leaned in, being pulled not from desire or heat, but ache.

Their first kiss was quiet and slow. The kind of kiss that asked permission and gave forgiveness in the same breath. His fingers slid behind her neck. She leaned into him more. The soft press of their lips that had known restraint too long. His hands traveled her back, hers slid up his chest.

As they leaned apart, she looked down, shy in the moment.

"I should probably feel worse," she whispered. "But I don't."

Donald cupped her jaw gently, guiding her eyes back to him.

"I do," he said. "But I'm here anyway."

"I didn't bring anything," she said softly. "No plan. No story. Just me."

"That's all I ever wanted," Donald replied.

Their hands searched each other like old habits, trembling slightly from the weight of emotional and physical restraint finally giving way. They undressed slowly, without a performance. Their skin was revealed in inches between stolen kisses and ragged breathing; the wine forgotten.

This time was different. It was not urgent or frantic but slow and deliberate. Two people memorizing the lines of what they might regret tomorrow.

Her shirt hit the floor first, soft cotton landing with a whisper. Then his followed, peeled open by her unsure fingers, one trembling button at a time. Each layer they removed felt like peeling away the weight of everything they weren't supposed to feel. Between kisses, between gasps, were pauses full of breathless tension. Moments where their eyes spoke truths their mouths couldn't say, yet.

His hand slid up the inside of her thigh, slow and methodical, until she shivered beneath his palm. He was tracing a map he'd only touched once before, other than in the quiet, guilty places in his head. His fingers pressed into her softness, reacquainting themselves with every give, every flutter, every tremor. She moaned low in her throat as her legs parted, and her hand slipped down, steady and sure, until her fingers wrapped around his cock.

She stroked him gently at first, as if savoring the heat of his dick in her palm. Then firmer, more rhythm than hesitation, more want than fear. His groan was raw, his head tipping forward to rest against hers while his hips twitched. He whispered her name like it was the only thing anchoring him.

"Kristal...that feels fucking amazing."

"You feel amazing," she breathed as she gripped his arm with her other hand.

Donald's fingers continued to explore her pussy with the moisture building. A slight squish from the suction action made Donald smile. His thumb circled her clit while two fingers pushed deep, curling inside her until her breath hitched and her hips rolled to meet him.

Their mouths met again, open, messy and hungry. Donald pushed Kristal back onto the bed. He straddled her, but she kept him right there, the thick head of his cock nudging at her entrance but not giving in.

"You're teasing me, Kristal," he rasped.

"Maybe I like hearing you beg," she murmured

Her thighs squeezed his hips, holding him like a lock.

Donald's jaw clenched as he traced his fingers over her hip, up her side, and caught her nipple between his thumb and forefinger. He rolled it gently at first, then tugged until she moaned.

"You're killing me," he muttered.

"Good," she whispered back, biting her lip as she rocked her hips just enough to slide his tip up against her clit. The slow grind made her shiver, a sweet ache blooming low in her belly.

Donald groaned, his hands braced on either side of her, the muscles in his arms taut. "You're so fucking wet."

Her answer was a low, satisfied hum as she reached down between them, wrapping her fingers around his shaft.

She stroked him, letting her thumb drag over the slick head, spreading pre-cum down his shaft in slow, teasing passes.

He pushed her hand away and slid his fingers between her thighs instead, dragging two through her folds until they were coated. He pressed his thumb and circled slow, just enough to make her hips twitch.

"Ohh, fuck..." she whispered, grabbing at his arm.

Donald leaned in, his mouth brushing the shell of her ear.

"I'm going to make you come before I'm even inside you."

"Okay," she rasped.

Her head tipped back as his thumb pressed harder, his fingers dipped into her in a deep, curling, rhythm that had her breath stuttering. She gasped, her body clenching around him as her first orgasm rolled through, sharp and fast, leaving her panting beneath him.

"What the fuck?!" She said with a smile.

Only then did he pull his hand away and grip himself, lining up with her soaked entrance.

He pushed in deliberately slow until the stretch made her eyes flutter shut, and her nails dug into his back.

"Fuck, you feel good," he groaned, savoring the embrace of her pussy around his dick.

Her moan was soft at first, then sharper as he pulled back and drove into her again, harder this time. Kristal whimpered, rolling her hips against his.

She tilted her head, lips grazing his ear as she whispered, breathless, "I didn't come here to be saved. I came because I wanted you. I want you to destroy me."

When he started to move, it was steady at first with long strokes that dragged his shaft through her, each thrust brushing that spot inside that made her gasp.

Kristal's hands slid into his hair, pulling him down into a kiss that was all tongue, pressure, messy and urgent.

He picked up the pace, finding a rhythm that made the mattress shift against the headboard. The slap of skin against skin filled the room. Kristal met him move for move, her legs tightening around him, dragging him deeper each time he tried to sit up.

"You feel...fuck," she groaned, losing the rest of the sentence against his mouth. She gasped into his kiss.

The bed groaned under them. The mattress was cool but quickly warmed from skin, heat and breath. His lips trailed along her shoulder, collarbone, down the delicate curve of her large breasts. Her nails raked lightly down his back, then settled over his heart like she was holding on to something fragile and fading.

Donald shifted, sliding one hand down between them until his thumb found her clit. She jerked against him, the sudden jolt of pleasure sending her voice higher.

"Don't stop," she panted.

"Not a chance," he answered, his pace quickening, each thrust hitting deeper, sharper, until her nails dug crescents into his back.

"Come for me again," he demanded, his voice low and rough.

She broke apart under him, trembling and gasping his name as he drove into her.

"Donald...don't you...don't you stop. I'm about cum."

Her body tensed beneath him with a tight pulsing squeeze around his cock telling him she was right there. He didn't let up until she cried out, trembling through her orgasm.

Donald's rhythm stuttered, his breath caught, and with one last hard thrust, he buried himself deep.

A guttural sound ripped from his chest as every muscle in his body went taut.

His hands gripped her hips hard enough to bruise, holding her in place as he pulsed inside her, thick, hot spurts spilling with each shuddering jerk of his hips.

Kristal moaned as the warm creamy ropes filled her insides.

He let out a long, uneven groan as he pressed his forehead to her chest. The tendons in his neck stood out as the pleasure wrung him dry.

At first, Donald couldn't move. He just stayed there, twitching inside her, riding out every last wave until all he could do was breathe against her lips.

They stayed there for a while, bodies pressed together and breathless. Their sweat cooled in the air-conditioned room. The air was thick with sex and something heavier neither of them dared to name. The rest of the world stayed on the other side of those four walls, small and irrelevant, as their breathing slowly evened out.

The thin motel sheets were twisted at their waists. The quiet between them was deeper now. It wasn't empty, but full of everything they didn't say.

"You okay?" he asked eventually.

"I shouldn't have come," Kristal whispered.

"Well, I should've stopped you," Donald replied.

Neither moved.

The guilt didn't land like thunder. It came slower like rain that starts after the storm has already passed, soaking what's already ruined.

"But you know...this is the first thing that's felt real in a while." Kristal said.

Donald didn't answer.

"You're thinking about Terry aren't you?" she asked, not lifting her head.

Donald's pause gave her the answer.

"I think about everyone," he finally said. "That's the problem."

Kristal sat up, pulling the sheet across her bare chest. Her voice cracked, not with anger—but with burden.

"You know, we keep saying we're not bad people. But we keep doing shit that bad people do."

Donald nodded slowly. "Well, maybe we're just people...doing what we feel instead of what's right."

"Why me?" she asked.

He brushed a strand of hair behind her ear.

"Because you acknowledged me. I didn't even realize I was invisible until you. Why did you choose me? I'm getting in great shape, but not everything can be enhanced." He said fading to a whisper. The thought of how he couldn't measure up to Peter was burned into his mind.

"Ohh my God! It's not about size if that's what you're still thinking about. I told you all those months ago that sex and big dicks aren't all that matters to me. Was it nice, sometimes painful, sure. But, in the end, relationships are about more than that. Besides, you pack a pretty good punch yourself. And you lasted."

"Yeah, magic from a little bottle," he said with a chuckle, then kissed her forehead.

"Exactly, silly. Stop worrying about comparing yourself. I've done the comparisons, and you win, hands down," she said with a kiss to his chest.

Donald let out a soft laugh.

"Well, at least I've got endurance. Guess I'll add that to the resume."

Kristal's smile widened, and the tension melted. They didn't fall asleep right away. Their bodies stayed humming, nerves alive, like the night wasn't done with them.

EPISODE: 19: Nia of It All

The night's heat still clung to the room, thick and stubborn. Donald sat at the edge of the bed, tugging on his jeans while Kristal moved around the room in nothing but an oversized T-shirt—his, from last night. Her hair was a mess of curls and sweat, her lips a shade darker than they'd started.

Neither of them said much.

The silence wasn't awkward, but it was loaded. The kind of silence that knows the taste of regret but hasn't swallowed it yet.

Kristal walked over to the mirror, swiping at her smudged eyeliner. "We really did it," she said softly.

Donald stood, pulling his hoodie over his head. "Yeah," he murmured, looking at her reflection in the mirror.

She slowly walked toward him, like she hadn't fully quenched the ache.

"What?" he asked, rougher than he meant.

Kristal hooked her fingers in his waistband before he could step back. She dropped to her knees, eyes looking into his.

"I just want to remember what it feels like," she whispered. "One more time."

Donald's hand found the wall, breath locking as she slid his pants down. Her mouth was warm, slow, and unhurried. The slow swirls of her tongue under his shaft as she slurped made Donald moan. He threaded his fingers through her curls as he called her name.

"Yes, Kristal. That's it."

She slid him deeper with every stroke, wet and relentless, until he tickled the back of her throat. She didn't flinch but welcomed it. Her cheeks gripped him tighter as she swallowed him deeper, her tongue lashing under his shaft as her throat gripped him tight. His hips bucked despite himself, and his voice cracked out of him before he could stop it.

"Fuck, Kristal, don't stop. Don't you dare."

His hand tightened in her hair, not pulling her away, but holding her there as if he needed her and this. His thighs quivered under the onslaught of feeling her and sound of his rod being serviced. Then, the heat that was rising in him finally broke.

"Fuck, I'm cumming."

"Mmm," he heard her hum back.

He groaned her name through his teeth as his stomach clenched.

"Shit, Kristal."

Heat surged through him, and then he was spilling into her mouth, hot, thick and pulsing. She swallowed the first gush, then the next, milking him with her mouth, her tongue stroking the underside of his shaft trying to drain him to the last drop.

"Oh, God...you're gonna kill me—" he gasped, his head tipping back, and whole-body shuddering as she kept sucking, teasing, refusing to let him go.

His cream coated her tongue, salty and heavy, but she didn't stop. She sucked him through the shudder, lips sealed around him, humming low until his knees nearly buckled

She finally eased off, pulling back with a wet pop. Her lips were glistening, and she dragged her tongue across them slowly, deliberately, like she was savoring the taste of him. She looked up at him, eyes serene, claiming him.

She kissed his hip and stood as Donald tugged his pants back up. He kissed her with one arm pulling her close.

Donald helped her pull on her coat without speaking. The moment between them said more than words. Neither of them mentioned love. Neither of them mentioned Terry. They just quickly checked out and slipped into the gray morning like two people trying to outrun their own shadows.

A few blocks away, Nia was settling into the vinyl chair at her favorite nail salon—Pink Pearl Nails & Spa. She always came early to avoid the Saturday crowd.

She scrolled through her phone, sipped green tea, and nodded to the nail tech without needing to speak. Halfway through a podcast on zodiac sex compatibility, she rolled her eyes at the claim that Aquarians were "emotional lovers" just as her phone buzzed.

Parking reminder.

She sighed, slipped on the disposable flip-flops, and carefully padded her way to the checkout desk.

"Y'all still take Zelle?"

The tech nodded. Nia paid, grabbed her keys, and slid her feet carefully into her slides. She was still walking delicately like she was carrying a secret between her toes.

As she stepped outside, the sunlight had broken through the clouds just enough to create that crisp morning glow. She blinked and reached for her sunglasses. It was there, across the parking lot, just past the motel entrance, she saw them.

Kristal was adjusting her jacket. Donald, brushing his hand through his hair like he was shaking off sin.

Nia didn't gasp.

She didn't flinch.

She just stopped walking and leaned slightly against her car door. It was all too damn obvious.

"Lord, these fools. I swear people don't know anything 'bout being discreet anymore," Nia thought as watched them.

Kristal's flushed face, Donald's limp face, the way they didn't speak, and how they existed side by side. It was like a neon sign flashing, "GUILTY."

Nia got in her car and waited until they got a few feet closer before she rolled down her window. They both stopped as they recognized her.

She looked at them, sunglasses reflecting their tangled guilt back at them.

"Well...damn. Guess subtlety's dead, huh? Y'all really went off-script...Better be careful."

Kristal's face blanched and Donald stood frozen for a few seconds. Finally, he cleared his throat.

"Nia...don't tell Terry. Please."

Nia's lips curved into a slow smirk. She leaned back in her seat, one hand casually on the wheel, then rolled the window up without another word. Kristal and Donald exchanged a glance before walking toward the corner.

Nia pulled out, her car gliding away as if she'd just left the scene of a crime she had no intention of reporting, at least not yet.

"She won't tell Terry," he said, mostly to himself. "Not directly anyway."

But they both knew better.

***

Kristal:

"Can we talk? Just us. At the park. I'll bring the yoga mats. You bring whatever."

Terry:

"Sure. It starts in one hour. Don't waste it." Terry replied after staring at the message for a few minutes.

The park was deceptively peaceful.

Morning sun filtered through Spanish moss and trembling dogwoods, casting lacework shadows across the worn brick path. A dozen yoga mats were already scattered in the grass, women stretching, chatting softly, the air filled with eucalyptus oil and quiet effort.

Terry stood near the edge of the group, arms crossed, sunglasses on, face blank. She hadn't come to find her center. She came for answers.

Kristal arrived five minutes late, barefoot, her rolled-up mats under one arm. Her face held that same fragile hope from Maine, the one Terry used to mistake for innocence.

Terry didn't wave. She didn't even nod. She just stared until Kristal drifted over, setting the mats beside her, quietness prickling between them.

"Thanks for coming," Kristal said, voice low.

"You said you wanted to talk," Terry replied flatly. "So fucking talk."

Kristal swallowed. "Look, I didn't come to fight."

"Then what do you want? And don't lie to me."

Kristal winced.

Terry shifted her weight, arms tightening.

“Are you sleeping with him?”

Kristal looked away.

“I...no. Not technically.”

“Not technically?” Terry stepped closer. Her voice rose just enough to turn a few heads.

Kristal’s voice dropped to a whisper.

“I kissed him. Once. We both did. But I didn’t come here to confess that. I came to tell you the truth.”

"Truth?" Terry laughed a dry, sharp exhale that didn’t reach her eyes. "You wanna talk truth now? After everything?"

"Look Terry, I’m not proud of how things happened. But I’m not going to lie anymore, either."

“Ohh, great. Now’s the part where I get your version of honorable betrayal?”

Kristal straightened, shoulders squared.

“I love him, Terry. I think I’ve loved him since Maine. I just didn’t realize it until now.”

The words hung there, louder than the whisper that carried them.

“I think I fell for him in Maine,” Kristal pressed on. “I didn’t mean to. I tried not to. But I can’t lie anymore. Not to myself. Not to you. I thought about him, too much. Especially after Peter and I ended things. I figured time would fix it. But when I saw him walk into the beach house, my heart melted.”

Terry blinked, and her hand moved before thought caught up. The sound of the slap cracked through the park like a splitting branch.

Kristal’s head snapped sideways. She staggered back, cheek stinging beneath her palm, stunned, but only for a second.

Kristal returned a slap that landed just as hard.

What followed wasn't cinematic. It wasn't elegant. It was raw, chaotic, ugly.

They lunged at each other like wounded animals. Their fists grabbing hair, elbows slamming into ribs. They rolled across the yoga mats, kicking over water bottles, shrieks and curses blending with the startled gasps of strangers.

The yoga instructor yelled, "someone break them up!" as a woman in leggings screamed and backed away.

Terry's hoodie ripped at the shoulder. Kristal's lip split open, blood bright against her teeth. Dirt smeared across both as they tumbled onto the grass, grunting, pulling and swinging until two older women stepped in and pried them apart.

Kristal sat on the grass, breathing hard, holding her bleeding lip.

Terry stood over her, chest heaving, eyes burning.

"You don't get to claim him," she hissed.

Kristal wiped a smear of blood from her lip. "I didn't claim anything. I just stopped pretending."

"Stay the fuck away from him," she said. "From both of us."

"You think I did this without your help Terry? You are just as much a part of this as I am."

Terry didn't respond. She walked away, chin high, fists clenched, legs trembling.

There were no goodbyes or promises of resolution.

Kristal sat in the trampled grass, surrounded by knocked-over mats and onlookers pretending not to stare. She stood slowly, wiping sweat from her palms, and spitting blood from her mouth. For a moment, the only sound was wind through the trees and her ragged breath.

Then a woman whispered nearby, "I guess that's what they meant by hot yoga."

EPISODE: 20: Good Chocolate

The café was nearly empty, except for a sleepy barista restocking pastries and two students arguing over a shared laptop in the corner. Rain tapped softly against the windows, rhythmic and low like the world trying not to interrupt.

Terry sat in the booth by the back wall, hoodie pulled low, hands curled around a paper cup that had long gone cold.

Nia slid into the opposite seat like she'd done a hundred times before, dropping her bag in the seat. She didn't offer a hug, or smile, just her presence.

"Wow, you look like hell," Nia said flatly, studying her friend.

Terry gave a weak laugh.

"Good. At least I'm being consistent."

Nia unwrapped some chocolate, popped it into her mouth and chewed without rush. Terry watched her, almost grateful for the normalcy, until finally she sighed.

"I did something stupid," Terry admitted. Her voice was low, weighted. "In the park. With Kristal. We actually fought, like kids. Rolling in the grass, knocking shit over. It was nuts."

Nia blinked, then gave a short, incredulous laugh.

"Wait...seriously? You fought her?" She shook her head, lips curling into a smirk. "Did you do better than expected?"

Terry didn't respond, she just glared back at Nia.

"Damn. I mean rollin' in the grass and everything? How does Kristal look?"

Terry groaned, dragging her palms down her face.

"It wasn't my finest moment."

"No," Nia agreed, unwrapping another chocolate. "But it was authentic. Maybe it was something you needed." She leaned back, eyes narrowing. "You've been sitting on all this resentment, confusion, whatever it is for weeks. It had to come out somehow."

Terry looked away, the shame still fresh.

"Doesn't make it right. I wasn't supposed to react like that. I thought I was better than that. Stronger."

"Didn't say it did." Nia shrugged, her voice calm but sharp. "But you're human. And honestly? You've been so loyal to everyone else that you forgot to fight for yourself. Maybe this was overdue. Hell, maybe Miss Sunshine needed to get hit."

Terry finally met her eyes, a crooked smile tugging at her mouth.

"Guess I can cross 'brawl in a public park' off my bucket list."

"Please. That wasn't a brawl. That was two raccoons in yoga pants." Nia snorted. "You're not a fighter," Nia said, simply. "But that doesn't mean you don't have paws. Just...aim them better next time."

Terry let out a full smile, then her voice came low, and thoughtful. "I feel like my brain doesn't know what to do with this information. Like I'm stuck in fog."

"You probably are," Nia replied. "But you're hurt and betrayed. And that's normal as shit."

"It's not just the betrayal. It's the surprise. I spent so long thinking I was the only one who really saw Donald. That I was the only one who could love him through his awkward silences, his terrible jokes, the way he always overthinks before he speaks." Terry sighed. "I thought someone like Kristal would always look past him."

Nia leaned forward, resting her chin on her fist.

"And when she didn't?"

Terry's eyes glistened. "I realized I'd been looking past him, too. For a long time. I made him feel like an obligation. Like something I could put down and pick up whenever I felt like it."

There was a long pause before Nia responded.

"Sometimes the ones we take for granted are the ones we break without meaning to," she said softly. "But that doesn't mean they're not still broken."

Terry looked up then. Her lip quivered.

"I think part of why I was so angry is because she reminded me that he was worth loving all along." She whispered

Nia reached across the table and placed her hand gently over Terry's.

"Hey, don't beat yourself up for that. Just focus on the truth, that you saw something in him long before anyone else."

"Hmm. I guess that's a way to look at it." Terry replied. She lifted her mug and took a sip of cold coffee, grimacing as if it were punishment she deserved.

"Have you talked to Donald yet?" Nia asked softly.

"No. Not yet. Wasn't sure what to say." Terry set the mug down with a soft thud. "I thought about calling him early this morning, even rehearsed what I'd start with, but it all sounded wrong. So, I didn't."

Nia hesitated, her thumb brushing the rim of her own mug. She forced a small nod, but her stomach knotted. The image of Donald and Kristal slipping out of that motel flashed. She shifted in her seat, hoping Terry wouldn't notice the pause before she spoke again.

"Well...maybe waiting was the right call," Nia said carefully. "Sometimes silence says more than rushing into the wrong words."

Terry hesitated, weighing something heavier than the coffee in front of her.

"The irony of this whole thing is it makes me want to work on the marriage," she admitted quietly. "But I don't know if it's because I want to or because I'm jealous."

"Well, sometimes that jealousy can point us to what we actually want."

"Do you really believe that shit?" Terry asked, looking down at her hands.

"I don't know," Nia admitted. "Just saying, I think the guilt of everything is blending with jealousy. It might be confusing you or could be directing you. Either way, you should listen."

"Yeah, maybe."

"What do you want right now? Don't think. Just answer." Nia questioned.

"I want to know the truth. All of it. No more riddles. I want everything to go the way I wanted them to. I wanted him to fight for me, the same way I should've fought for him. But we both failed."

Nia studied her. "Sounds like you want closure. A concrete truth you can stand on even if it sinks the marriage."

Terry let out a dark chuckle. "A good drowning might be what our marriage needs."

"Start with honesty," Nia said. "With him and with yourself." Nia tipped her head toward the door. "Come on, let's go drown this bitch," she chuckled.

EPISODE: 21: The Cost

^Three weeks later...^

The group text thread, once buzzing with late-night memes and morning "what's the plan?" check-ins, had flatlined. No one responded to anything anymore. Event invites came and went, ghosted like old flames. The silence wasn't just digital, it felt spiritual. Heavy. Uneasy.

Julian's latest message sat there, unread by half the group:

"So, we not doing Friendsgiving this year? Just checking before I return this damn turkey."

No replies.

Nia followed up ten minutes later with her signature sass:

"Y'all are giving full-on code blue energy, and nobody's brave enough to call it. Don't make me crack the chest."

Still nothing.

The thread remained untouched by Kristal, Terry, Donald, or Peter. Not even read receipts.

Kristal saw the messages when they came through. She stared at them like they belonged to someone else's life. The people in that thread had shared beds, secrets, and laughter that once echoed in seaside kitchens and lakeside cabins. Now, they were ghosts haunting each other's phones.

Donald also read Julian's message but didn't react. He sat on the edge of his bed, phone in one hand, a glass of Macallan 25 in the other. The house was quiet. Even the hum of the refrigerator felt like judgment.

Across town, Terry stood over a box half-packed with winter coats. She had opened her laptop to respond, fingers hovering over the keys. But what would she say? "Sorry we destroyed our friend group with betrayal and sex?"

She closed it.

Peter didn't even look at the messages. He'd muted the group weeks ago, choosing instead to dive into gym sessions and casual flings that meant nothing but gave him everything.

None of them were ready. Not because they didn't care, but because they cared too much and too late.

In the vacuum of that unspoken pain, they all carried a shared truth: This wasn't just a fallout. It was a reckoning.

***

Kristal came over just after dark.

The sky was a blanket of navy. The wind was cool against her skin as she stepped onto Donald's porch. She paused before knocking. The porch light was off, but she saw the flicker of the TV through the living room window.

Donald opened the door like he'd been waiting with his hand on the knob.

Kristal smiled standing there, hair down, no makeup, sweatshirt hanging loose looking soft and tired.

"Hey," she said, voice soft but loaded.

His eyes dragged down her body and back up, like he had to remind himself she was real.

"You still want me?" she asked, her voice barely above a whisper.

"Wanting you was never the problem." Donald stepped aside, letting her in.

Kristal stepped inside and the space between them disappeared. The second the door shut, her back hit the wall. Donald's mouth crushed hers, rough and hungry, teeth catching her bottom lip hard enough to sting. She gasped, but he swallowed the sound, leaning into the wall. The kiss was messy, teeth and tongue, more like a bite than a welcome.

Her hands clawed at his shirt, dragging it over his head with her nails scraping his stomach. His chest was hot under her palms, muscles flexing as he pulled her sweatshirt off in one sharp motion. He bent, lips and teeth at her throat, sucking just below her jaw before biting down. He dragged his thumb along the underside of her large mounds until her knees nearly buckled.

"God, I missed this," she gasped against his lips. "Still want me?"

"I'm about to prove it," he growled.

His hand slid into her shorts, fingers finding her slick and ready. She arched, head hitting the wall, as he rubbed slow circles that made her thighs tremble. She grabbed at his wrist, not to stop him but to keep herself from collapsing.

"Fuck, Donald--"

He shoved her pants down, dropped to his knees, and buried his face between her thighs before she could finish the sentence. His tongue worked fast and relentlessly. The wet sounds echoed in the hall along with Kristal's moans. She clutched his hair, grinding against his mouth.

"Donald, I'm—" She broke off, the rest swallowed by the sharp cry that tore through her as she came, shaking under his mouth.

Before the aftershocks even faded, he stood, turned her, and bent her over the arm of the couch. His zipper hissed down in one quick flick. The blunt head of his cock pushed into her, stretching her wide in one hard thrust that punched a moan straight out of her chest.

"God, yes," she gasped, fingers gripping the cushion until her knuckles went white.

He fucked her deep and hard. The couch groaned with every drive of his hips. One hand on her waist, the other tangled in her hair, yanking her head back.

Kristal threw a look over her shoulder, voice sharp through ragged breaths.

"Harder. I want to feel you every time I sit down tomorrow."

"This pussy's going feel me tomorrow." He growled back.

His answer was met with a moan, cut off by her own teeth sinking into her lip as he drove her over the edge again. She came hard, shuddering, clenching and spilling over him until it coated his cock in a creamy mess. Every slap of their bodies turned wetter, filthier, smearing her release across his stomach as he drove into her. He kept grinding deeper, never slowing. He just pounded her through the orgasm, growling as he chased his own.

He slammed into her one last time, hips snapping hard as he spilled inside her, groaning low. The heat of him mixed with the slick mess that coated his cock and ran down her thighs in filthy streaks. He kept thrusting, pumping the last drops deep before finally collapsing back, chest heaving.

For a moment, the only sound was their ragged breathing, the couch creaking beneath them. Then Donald's hand went from a fist in her hair to a tender stroke on her back. He pressed a kiss to her shoulder, still inside her but softening, his voice rough and warm.

"Come on," he murmured, brushing his lips against her ear. "Let's take this somewhere better."

She let him guide her up, legs shaky, both of them slick and marked by what they'd just done. He laced their fingers together as they stumbled toward the bedroom, leaving the wreckage of the couch behind.

In the dim light, Donald paused at the dresser, tugging open a drawer for a clean towel. He pressed it gently between her thighs, catching the mess, his touch softer now. An apology hidden in every careful swipe. Kristal took it from him halfway, dabbing herself, their eyes locking in the silence.

Neither of them spoke. Instead, she pulled back the sheets, the cool cotton brushing her skin as she slipped beneath it. Donald sat on the edge of the bed for a moment, elbows braced on his knees, running a hand over his face like he wasn't sure if he deserved to follow her in..

When he finally lay beside her, the room seemed smaller. The mood wasn't frantic anymore. It was calm with choices made, with things neither of them had to say out loud.

That was how they started again, not with frenzy, but with hesitance. With the kind of touches that lingered too long, like both of them were testing the strength of something already cracked.

Kristal kissed him like she was afraid it might be the last time. Donald touched her like he was trying to memorize what regret felt like.

She kissed her way down every inch of his chest. Her fingers curled around him, tender and possessive, like she was holding a memory.

Donald groaned low in his throat, his hands finding her shoulders, her name whispered like confession.

"Kristal."

She moved with purpose, slow and intimate, not for performance but connection. When he pulled her back up and into his arms, it was a seamless transition from hunger to admiration, almost primal.

Kristal got on top of Donald. He was engorged, ready for another session with her. She eased down on his cock like a puzzle piece that had always belonged, even if the picture made no sense.

They made love like they were trying to rebuild something. The rhythm was gentle, almost humble. The bedroom was a cocoon of half-light and soft sounds. Kristal's moans curled into his ear, her nails dragging just enough to leave ghost trails across his chest.

They moved like people who didn't want to be forgiven, only remembered. Slow. Careful. Bittersweet.

Kristal rocked harder against him, chasing it, her breath breaking against his mouth. Donald held her hips, guiding her, his own body trembling with the effort to keep steady. When she cried out, dragging her nails over his chest, he followed, groaning into her shoulder.

The crash of climax left them clinging, sweat-slick and shaking, hearts pounding out of sync. For a moment it was everything, hot, overwhelming, and all-consuming.

Then came the aftermath. The kind that stretched, dense but soft, as their bodies stilled and their breaths slowly fell into rhythm.

Donald brushed a strand of hair from her face, his thumb lingering on her cheek. Kristal pressed her lips to his palm, her eyes searching his like she wanted to hold on but wasn't sure if she could.

They stayed like that, in the dark, both of them knowing the moment couldn't fix anything but only make sure it was remembered.

Afterward, tangled in the sheets, she lay with her head on his chest, listening to the rhythm of a heart that began to beat for her.

They sat there quietly until it was too much to hold. Donald broke the silence first.

"What happens to us now?"

Kristal let out a shaky laugh, her cheek still pressed to his chest.

"It was just supposed to be a vacation."

Donald's hand traced a slow path down her back.

"I know. Turns out we packed too much stuff and not enough common sense."

"That night in Maine changed everything, didn't it? I saw you there, and you noticed me for me. Not just something to be conquered." She tilted her head, her voice softer now.

His hand stilled, resting warm against her side.

"Yeah," he murmured, voice low. "And I've been trying to unsee it ever since."

Kristal's breath brushed against his skin.

"Me too." She didn't move away, though every nerve told her she should.

The truth between them pressed closer than their bodies. Terry's name wasn't spoken, but it pulsed there, unyielding, in the room.

The evening wasn't perfect, but for the first time in days, neither of them felt alone.

A low hum broke through the peace.

Donald stiffened before the headlights cut across his yard. The sound wasn't just any car; it was Peter's SUV, sleek and expensive, its growl unmistakable.

"Peter?" Kristal whispered.

"Yeah, I think so." Donald nodded, jaw set. "Stay here."

He pushed himself from the bed, leaving the warmth of her body behind. Kristal drew into the shadows of the bedroom, heart pounding against her ribs as the front door creaked open.

Peter stepped out his SUV, crisp as ever. Fresh fade, designer shirt, shoes gleaming like a star. He smelled like cologne and confrontation.

Donald shut the glass door behind him, standing on the porch like a wall. He didn't invite him in.

Peter's smile was sharp and humorless.

"Figured I'd come see you eventually. You've been ghosting me. Thought maybe Kristal had your phone. Or your balls."

Donald didn't flinch.

"Why would she have either? Plus, it's none of your fucking business."

The porch went still.

EPISODE: 22: The Final Boss

Donald and Peter stood there for a long, tense moment. Kristal watched through a sliver of curtain, the light carving both men into statues.

"You always been that dude. The slow burn. Then one day you light a fire nobody can put out."

Peter stepped forward slowly. Each step was deliberate. He stopped at the edge of the porch, and they mirrored stances, arms folded, shoulders squared like two alpha wolves sniffing out the boundary line.

"I know you wanted her since Maine," Peter continued. "You can't deny it. You just let it marinate. Real slick."

Donald's jaw tightened.

"You talk like you fucking know me. But you don't. Not like that."

Peter smirked, shifting his weight.

"Bitch, please. I watched you watch her. The long looks, the way you'd back off soon as me or Terry walked in the room. That ain't friendship, that's patience. Big difference."

Donald's eyes narrowed.

"Patience is knowing the difference between wanting something and taking it before its time. But your dumbass don't know that word."

Peter chuckled low, but there wasn't any humor in it.

"Nah. See, I don't waste time circlin'. I go for what's mine."

Donald tilted his head, studying him like he'd finally seen the crack in the armor.

“This isn’t about Kristal or me, is it? It’s Terry. You wanted her. Still do. But she doesn’t want you, and that's eating at you. So now you bring all this bullshit to my door.”

For a second Peter’s smirk faltered. His jaw worked, teeth grinding, before he snapped back, voice rougher.

“Don’t twist this. You had both. Both. And for what? You? The guy who couldn’t look in a mirror without flinchin’? The guy we all had to drag out his own head? You're not better than me,” Peter said, eyes burning. “You never were. But by some fucking miracle, they chose you. That’s what I can’t stomach.”

Donald’s jaw tightened.

“Don’t blame me for what you ruined. You had Kristal, and you burned that down with your own ego. Big dick and all, you still don’t know what to do with someone who actually needs love.”

“Love? Fuck that shit. She made me feel like a god in bed but like a ghost when the sun came up. But now? I can’t even have the woman who I was supposed to be with. And you think what... just because you read poetry and take long walks, you got her figured out?”

“No,” Donald said. “But I listened. And I cared. And that was more than you ever did, apparently.”

Peter stepped closer, his eyes hard under the streetlight.

“She chose you. Fine. But don’t act like you didn’t break the whole damn thing to get there. Because I’ll never understand how someone like you ends up with everything I wanted.”

Donald didn’t move. He let the words settle, then said quietly, “we all broke it. The difference is I admitted it. Stopped pretending I could tape over the pieces. Don’t bring your bullshit over here because you can't get what you want. That has nothing to do with me. Terry looked at you and decided you weren't good enough either."

The streetlight buzzed. Peter stepped in, close. A porch board strained, but Donald held his ground and met his eyes.

Peter's fist curled; the keys dug into his palm. Donald was ready for whatever came next. Then, Peter swallowed the urge. He turned for the SUV, kicked the rear tire, and yanked the door open; his knuckles flashed red. The door slam cracked the still of the night. The engine purred to life, leaving behind the echo of everything unsaid.

Donald stood still as the fading engine hum and Peter's taillights disappeared. Alone again, he exhaled and turned toward the dark window where Kristal waited.

He felt the weight pressing lighter on his chest than before.

***

^Two Days Later...^

The house was almost empty now.

Terry moved quietly, methodically, packing the last of her things. The house felt like an echo, hollow, stripped of warmth with only fragments of the life they'd built here. She stopped and staired at a photo of her and Donald before they left for their honeymoon. The image almost caused a waterfall of tears, but she didn't let herself think. She just packed.

The books from the shelves went first, her favorite novels that Donald had once teased her about, now tucked into cardboard boxes. Next went clothes, shoes, even the mugs she'd collected over years of coffee-filled mornings and whispered conversations. She wrapped each mug in paper, gentle with each memory, sealing them away one by one.

No music played. No distractions. Just the soft thud of items dropping into boxes.

She had nearly finished when her spare charger fell and landed beneath the couch. She reached for it and her fingers brushed something thin.

She pulled it out and stared. It was a small, black hair tie, with a stretched band and one lone bright hair threaded through it. In that moment she knew it was Kristal's.

Terry's hand shook, her breathing suddenly uneven. She rolled it between her fingers and snapped it against her palm. The sight of it was like a sharp knife, reopening the wound she'd temporarily sewn shut. Anger rushed in first, hot and immediate but beneath it was grief. It rose silently, painfully, tears slipping down her cheeks before she could stop them.

She sank to the floor, legs folded beneath her, gripping the hair tie so tightly it left an impression on her palm. The tears were quiet, no sobbing, just a relentless, silent stream of hurt. She remembered when this had been their place, when laughter filled the silence, not emptiness.

Eventually, her breathing slowed. She stood, wiping her face with the back of her hand, forcing composure back into her expression. Terry walked into the bedroom, eyes landing on the framed Vegas photo from their anniversary. It was a happier time; one she couldn't reconcile with the current moment. She picked it up, smiles frozen behind glass, a poignant reminder of a different reality. Terry carried it carefully to the kitchen and placed it face-up beside the keys on the counter.

Then she pulled out the note she wrote earlier. The words rehearsed in her head countless times but still painful to read now. Her handwriting was firm yet vulnerable on the page:

I loved you more than I showed you. And I'm sorry for that.

I forgive you.

I just can't forgive myself for giving Kristal the option of you.

With one last glance around the room, a final aching farewell, she switched off the lights. Evening shadows consumed what was left of their shared history.

When she closed the door behind her, it wasn't loud. But the soft click echoed with decisiveness louder in her heart than any shouting ever could.

***

^Three Weeks Later...^

The rooftop was high enough to feel removed from the chaos below but close enough that the city's lights twinkled quietly in the distance, like half-hearted promises.

Kristal sat curled up on the worn wooden bench, wrapped in one of Donald's oversized hoodies, knees tucked to her chest. Her hair moved in the breeze, strands lifting and falling. She stared out over the city, trying to pinpoint when everything had become so complicated.

Donald climbed the stairs slowly, holding two steaming cups of coffee. He set one beside her on the bench, then eased himself down, careful to leave enough space that the tension between them wouldn't snap too soon.

She glanced at the cup. "Decaf?"

"Regular. I figured neither of us was getting much sleep anyway."

Kristal laughed softly, shaking her head.

"True. Might as well stay awake and worry about our terrible choices in crystal-clear focus."

"If we're talking choices, I think it's safe to say we've both made worse." Donald chuckled.

Kristal raised an eyebrow.

"Speak for yourself. I'm pretty sure fucking and falling for my best friend's husband tops the charts."

Donald winced, then shrugged.

"Fair. I still remember that you killed the last of the rosé and tried to teach us a 'quiet twerk' so Peter wouldn't notice."

Kristal groaned, burying her face briefly in her hands.

"It was a controlled demonstration."

"Nothing about that was controlled," he said, smiling.

"At least nobody called the cops."

"They probably tried," he said, "couldn't find the house. Terry tried to do it and looked even worse."

With the mention of her name, their laughter faded, leaving a thinner, truer quiet neither wanted to disturb.

"Do you think we'll ever be okay?" Kristal asked.

Donald took a slow sip of coffee, looking out at the scattered lights.

"Honestly? I don't know. Still have shit to deal with. You know the divorce. Terry texted me and said no reason for lawyers or anything."

She nodded, accepting that uncertainty.

“Me either. But I don’t regret it. I do miss my friend, but sometimes...life is just weird, I guess.”

"Yeah, it is. Never thought I'd be here with someone else, hoping for a good life. I mean, if that’s what you want."

"Donald, I don’t ever want you to let me go."

Donald’s fingers brushed hers lightly. She turned her palm upward, letting their fingers lace together, warmth spreading slowly between them.

“At least we’re not lying anymore,” Donald said quietly.

“Yeah. There’s that.” Kristal squeezed his hand.

They sat for a long time, watching the city breathe beneath them, lights flickering, distant sirens whispering secrets neither would ever know.

Finally, Donald turned to her, eyes serious but soft. “We broke a lot of things, didn’t we?”

“We did,” Kristal replied, unapologetic.

He hesitated, thumb stroking her knuckles. “Think it’s fixable? I mean, think we can survive this together?”

Kristal leaned into him, her voice barely above a whisper.

“I think...it's already broke. But maybe what’s left is something we build new, not fix. Not the same love. Not the safe kind. The kind that knows what it costs and still chooses to stay. If you’re still choosing me then yeah. I think we survive.” She looked up at him. “And I’m choosing you. Even if it’s messy.”

He blinked, like her words struck someplace he hadn’t let himself hope for.

“Then let’s build it,” he said, low and steady. “Brick by broken-ass brick. I’m choosing you too. Not because it’s easy.

Cause it sure as hell is not. But because I can't picture any version of peace that doesn't have you in it."

Their lips met gently at first, then deeper, kissing like people that knew exactly what they stood to lose and had chosen it anyway. The night air wrapped around them, a silent witness to what they made in darkness but finally faced openly, beneath the stars.

The rooftop offered no easy promises.

Just the quiet comfort of honesty.

And, for now, that was enough.

EPISODE: 23: What Remains

POV: Nia

The nail salon was half-empty, acetone and lavender lotion hanging in the air. Nia sat in the corner chair, legs up, sipping a glass of Prosecco the tech said was "complimentary, not optional."

Her phone buzzed.

Julian:

"We really done done, huh?"

She sighed, set down her glass, and thumbed a reply.

Nia:

"This group fell apart like lace panties in a gas dryer. Shame. We had better tension than most Netflix originals."

She followed it up with a meme of a burning friendship bracelet wrapped around a bottle of whiskey, then waited. The typing bubble popped up. Then vanished. Then came back.

Julian:

"I miss them. Even the drama. Even Peter's loud-ass laugh."

Nia:

"Same. I miss Donald's dumb jokes and Terry pretending to hate 'em. I even miss Kristal's side-eye every time one of us said something inappropriate."

Julian:

"You think they'll be able to be cordial?"

Nia stared at the screen, biting her lip. The tech gently nudged her toe, motioning for her to relax. She leaned back in the chair, still typing.

Nia:

"I think they're all too prideful. Too wounded. But I know from experience that's what love does—burns bright, leaves scars, and makes you wish you handled the flame better."

Julian replied with a broken heart emoji, then a gif of someone pouring wine into a soup bowl.

Julian:

"Pour one out for the group. We had a good run."

Nia:

"Not dead. Just dormant. Like herpes."

Julian's laugh emoji hit instantly. Nia smirked, half-listening to the woman next to her rant about an ex, half-watching reliving her own painful journey that Terry helped her through.

POV: Terry

The new apartment was small but clean. Roses and cedar scented the room. A simple painting hung a little crooked. Terry tried to straighten it but eventually let it be.

She sat on the edge of her new bed, staring at a half-folded pile of sweaters, her thoughts trailing backward like a thread being pulled.

She hadn't meant to hurt Donald. Not at first. But over time, her jokes stopped being funny and started being sharp. She used to tease Donald about his belly, about falling asleep after sex, about how he needed GPS to find her G-spot.

He laughed with her, until he didn't.

What she'd written off as banter had chipped his confidence. The man she came home to shrank under her words even as he tried to love her harder. More flowers. More chores. More effort.

And then, he changed.

The gym became his sanctuary. He got leaner. Stronger. Started wearing cologne again. She caught him checking himself in the mirror and hated that it made her jealous. When he started using those pills, she couldn't pretend not to notice the newfound swagger in his step or the way other women started noticing too.

She resented it, quietly. The new body, the confidence, the way he started moving through the world like he didn't need her approval anymore.

Terry stared at her phone, focused on Donald's name. Her heart thudded against her ribs like it was trying to get out and chase him down.

She started typing:

"I miss you. I don't know how things got so bad."

She paused.

Deleted it.

Started again:

"You deserved better. I see that now. I see you now."

Her finger hovered over the send button.

Then she stopped, breathing through the ache in her chest.

"I didn't just lose him," she whispered, staring at the glowing screen. "I made him someone I can't reach anymore."

She locked the phone and set it face down on the table.

Not today.

But maybe one day.

POV: Peter

Rooftop restaurant. Old fashioned in hand, laughing on cue. Across from him sat his date with long legs, high heels, and an Instagram following that could fund a lifestyle.

"My aura's wrecked from Mercury retrograde," she said.

Peter nodded absently, sipping his old fashioned.

"Like, I can't even explain it. I just can feel when people are energetically toxic. And by the way, I only eat purple foods on Thursdays. It's a vibration thing."

He blinked. Once. Twice.

To him, her voice grated like steel on a mirror. The fake laugh. The self-diagnosed star seed energy. The unsolicited astrology breakdown. It was all too much.

But she was sexy and already ordered dessert. And truth be told, Peter didn't want to go home alone.

So, he smiled.

"Wanna get outta here?"

She lit up.

"I thought you'd never ask!"

He held the door open, already tuning her out again.

She wasn't Kristal. She wasn't Terry. She wasn't even interesting.

But she'd do for tonight.

On the way down, he took his phone out in the elevator. He looked over a name he'd thought about deleting and stared at his own reflection in the black glass. Then, he slid it back into his pocket.

The fire under that Maine sky didn't go out; it changed shape—into scars, into silence, into the small, stubborn things that remain.

www.ingramcontent.com/pod-product-compliance
Lightning Source LLC
LaVergne TN
LVHW090942080826
845145LV00003B/855

* 9 7 8 1 7 3 6 5 9 1 3 9 0 *